Cold Guns

A few years after the Civil War, Lou Hollister returns to Texas, bearing the cruel scars of an enemy prison stockade. Once home, he thinks he can settle and cast off a threatening and beleaguered past. Instead, he finds a family without hope, and a ranch manipulated by Tusk Tenbridge, the corrupt sheriff of Cottonwood County.

From the squalid cow-town of Toya Bend, back to the New Mexico Railhead at Ciudad Blanco, Lou fights to regain his ranch and the last of its cattle. When a great snowstorm surges in from the Sacramento Mountains, it falls across the burnt-out remains of Pasedera Ranch. It is here that Lou must confront his tormentors from the past. Can he now wreak his final, bloody revenge?

Cold Guns

CALEB RAND

A Black Horse Western

ROBERT HALE · LONDON

ISBN 0 7090 7470 0

Robert Hale Limited
Clerkenwell House
Clerkenwell Green
London EC1R 0HT

Typeset by
Derek Doyle & Associates, Liverpool.
Printed and bound in Great Britain by
Antony Rowe Limited, Wiltshire

1

CIUDAD BLANCO

Twenty miles north of the Texas border, between the Sacramento mountains and the Pecos River, thin trails of smoke lifted from the chimneys of the low-slung buildings of Ciudad Blanco. Late in the year, it was a cold and raw, end of line town that offered little in the way of comfort. But Lou Hollister didn't mind, he was on his way somewhere else and wasn't much interested.

It was after first dark when he crossed the rail track. Lou was rangy, but toughly built, and rode easily in his saddle. He wore poke spurs, and the toe-spiders of his boots worked lightly in the stirrups. As he turned into the main street, a breezy wind snatched aside a fold of his coat to reveal his long-barrelled Colt.

Ahead of him was the stagecoach depot, and a sheriff's office. To the side was a livery stable and blacksmith's shop. Set back, beyond the cow pens, were the tents and hurdy-gurdies which offered diversions of whoring, gambling and gunplay. For trail-weary cowboys Ciudad Blanco was where law and order didn't get in the way of spicy pleasures.

Lou crabbed the horse across the mudded ruts and up to the steps of a saloon. On one side of the door NATHAN'S GAP was branded into the clapboarding. He looked at his sorrel mare and nodded at the loose hitch. It was only a signal of restraint and he held up the palm of his hand.

'Maybe I'll play me some cooncan. Don't *you* go gettin' into any trouble,' he said.

In Nathan's the smells of tobacco and oaked-whiskey mingled with the pungent tang of cattle-herders. There were five or six tables, and each one had a fat lard candle burning in the centre, but like most of southern New Mexico, everything appeared to be washed out, lightly floured.

Lou walked slowly to the bar, took off his faded grey cap, and asked the bartender for a beer. He guessed it might be a mistake, changed his mind and settled for whiskey. He lifted a tortilla from a wooden platter and dunked a fragment into the rough spirit. For anyone interested, this was him taking his supper. He stared into the back-bar mirror for a while, until he made contact with the reflections of two men sitting behind him.

One of them was a young Mexican, swarthy, with dull black eyes. A livid scar curled from the side of his left eye to his left nostril. But the other man had a sallow face and long, waxy-coloured hair; his eyes had the cast of someone who harmed for pleasure.

There was a bottle of whiskey on the table and two glasses. For a long time, the older man looked back at the reflection of Lou before he spoke. He rubbed his mouth and nose against the sleeve of his coat, insensible to the trail of mucus that stretched from wrist to elbow.

'Hey, feller. Don't I know you from somewhere?' he called. 'Turn around an' let me see you, proper.'

Lou turned and looked at both men with apparent lack of concern.

The man's voice was charged with goading.

'Yeah, you got yourself dried out now, though – got out o' that Southern livery.'

A nerve at the corner of Lou's right eye twitched. His stance hardened but he remained silent.

The Mexican grinned nastily. 'Looks like he ain't goin' to bite, Org?'

Organ Chimm showed his quid-stained teeth.

'Sure he is. Just needs to have the bait jiggled.' He unwound himself from the table and stepped forward.

When the man approached him, Lou realized he was pushing for a fight.

'Baton Rouge in '62, or was it Natchez? I sort o' recognized that old peaked sunhat o' yours. There was hundreds of 'em. Floated like lily-pads they did, down that goddamn Mississippi. It was all we ever saw o' you cowardly John Rebs until we fished you out.'

At the mention of Natchez, a haunting shudder ran through Lou. Natchez was where Union gunboats had broken the defending Rebel force. He spoke with a thin, scornful smile across his face.

'An' I recognize your mouth. It reminds me o' the hole in the ground I spent a lot o' time squattin' over.'

Chimm moved in close, but the Mexican was suddenly behind him, holding him back, his scar tight and livid.

'You're right about Org's mouth, *amigo*. Gets us both into no end o' trouble.'

As memories of the Confederate defeat returned to haunt and trouble Lou, Chimm shook away the Mexican's restraining arm.

'That's some cannon you're keepin' warm, cotton-seed. Not goin' to object to me takin' a closer look, are you?'

'I probably will,' was Lou's quiet warning, but Chimm took no heed.

As Chimm reached for the Colt, Lou drove the point of his elbow up and into the man's mouth. Chimm didn't make a sound, other than a short, mushy grunt. In the same instant, Lou lashed out with his foot at the Mexican who was leaving the gun-taking to Chimm. He was surprised by Lou's retaliation, and only had time to stare. Lou's foot caught him low in the belly and, as he folded, Lou snapped his left arm around his neck. He wrenched hard, using the man's body as a shield. He staggered two steps backward, trying to see what Chimm, or the barman, or anyone else was going to do. With a crushing throat and a busted gut, the Mexican was turning into a dead weight. Lou loosed him, and with his right hand swung up his gun.

As the man crumpled at his feet, Lou fired a shot

across the bar. The bullet sent the tortillas flying, then the whiskey bottle and a cluster of empty glasses. Scared for his life, the barman had retreated in the uproar. The few remaining customers gaped and sat, fearful, at their tables.

Chimm lunged awkwardly at Lou, but slipped in the spilled booze and smashed glass. He cursed, and pitched head first into a chair and across a table. The Mexican choked, and from the floor, raised his gun. But he was used up, and as his finger curled to the trigger, his wrist was slammed by the barrel of Lou's Colt.

Lou made for the the door, kneeing the side of Chimm's head in his dash to the street. The sorrel was standing, nervous but ready, and Lou threw himself into the saddle. He drove his heels deep into the horse's flanks, and at the end of the main street, he swung east. He thought about his imminent return to Texas, and set off in an unrestrained gallop. It was time to get to the border.

2

THE PREY

Ever since he'd crossed the Pecos River, Lou knew he was being trailed. They'd stayed far off, keeping distance, but Lou was tired of their grinding presence, tired of looking to his back, and chilly nights without a camp-fire. He hoped to make the border the following day, or early the one after. That was when his pursuers would make a try for him, if they really meant business. On the outskirts of the llano, law enforcement was usually down to who pulled a trigger first.

Lou couldn't think of any reason why he should be hunted. There'd been a minor skirmish in Fort Hancock, even a reward out for him for a while, but that was a few years back. The man who'd tried to collect had ended his life face down in the Salt Flats.

Towards the end of a long, dry scrape, Lou dismounted. He left his horse nosing dirt, while he crawled up the bluffed slope. He hunkered down, held the brim of his cap against the big sky. To the east, the plateau levelled hard and colourless. There was nothing that moved, and he turned his attention west.

A mile in the distance, a dry wash curled between low ridges, its course marked by gnarled shrub and bunchgrass. As he watched, a peppery cloud burst from a stand of spiky willow. It was what Lou needed to know, and he scrambled more positively back down the bluff. Those who were still following had just scared a few scrub jays from their concealed squat.

Lou was safe enough for a while, and he let the sorrel off at a canter. They wouldn't approach him before dark, so that gave him plenty of time to ponder their identities. They could be goodwill travellers, keeping out of sight because that was a good idea. A lot of folk moved around that way when they found themselves west of Houston or Dallas. They either weren't looking for trouble, or they'd already found it.

But somehow Lou didn't think so. During the last two days he'd changed direction half a dozen times, but still they trailed him. A sense of foreboding scratched at his vitals and again he thought about his return to Texas. He wondered whether anyone knew about what had happened to him, where he'd been. It wasn't likely that any flag-waving Texan would express sympathy or understanding. The brawl he'd endured in Cuidad Blanco was a reminder, and he wondered how long it would be before the next conflict.

*

For nearly ten miles they galloped, until they met the sharp, chill breezes that drifted across the plain, then they slowed to a walk until the very last of the day's light had slipped away. Lou dismounted and let the reins drop from his fingers. He walked into the cold, blue night, felt the soft touch of the sorrel's nose between his shoulder blades. At that moment it was the touch of *camaraderie* he needed.

He had supper for him and his horse, and there was water from the Pecos gully. He broke up an apple for the horse, and for himself, bacon and bread and coffee over a dare-devil fire. He was getting some warmth into him before doing something about being prey. When he'd eaten, he set about fixing his bedroll. He pressed a saddle-pouch and dry mesquite under the blanket, and set his old cap high against the skirt of his saddle. Against the dying embers of his camp-fire, and under the thin moonlight, the deception looked believable from a dozen paces or more.

Lou looked cautiously around him. It was full dark, and a lone coyote howled from far across the plain. After checking his ammunition he led the sorrel off a short distance. He made a loose hobble, then moved back to the far side of the dying fire. He kicked out a hide in the brush and, resting the gun in the crook of his arm, he curled up and waited.

Three of them came soon after midnight. Two rode together and one kept his distance. They were within thirty feet of the fire when the sorrel sniffed them out. It curled its lips and let out a screaming whinny.

Lou withered as the fusillade of gunshots broke the night apart. In the gunflashes he saw the two men he'd tangled with in Cuidad Blanco. But he had no time to think on it as they spurred their horses forward.

From where he was holed up, Lou heard the young Mexican shout:

'It'll be a cold night in the lower regions before he wakes, Tusk. Reckon we hit him three, four times.'

There was a low response from the man who remained further back in the darkness. 'Don't take no chances, Rido. I can't risk one o' them Hollisters turnin' up,'

The mention of his own name had Lou immediately confused and shaken. He squinted, his eyes aching to see more clearly. Chimm sat a big grey, and he held a Winchester. The Mexican followed him closely with a handgun.

Both men pulled up just outside the glow of the tine. Chimm shook his head, anxiously.

'Today's molehills are tomorrow's mountains,' he said, and watched the Mexican fire another two rounds into the bundle that was Lou Hollister.

In the crushed, still silence that followed, Lou minced at the sweet, acrid bite of powder-smoke that eddied around his face. He watched spellbound as Chimm rammed the barrel of his rifle into the inert form; gripped his Colt even tighter, as the tall, white-haired man yelled wretchedly into the night.

'It's not him! The greyback ain't here. It's just a bundle o' rags.'

Lou stood and fired then. 'You miserable scum,'

he yelled. It was too dark for him to make a killing shot, but it was close, and Chimm dashed the grey away in alarm. Lou fired and shouted again, but the horse and rider were already lost to the night.

Lou dropped to one knee. The Mexican was holding his horse on a tight rein as it snorted and bucked. Lou could see that in remaining, the youngster had some inbred grit. The Mexican gripped his horse tightly with his legs and, backing slightly, fired two quick shots deliberately at Lou.

They fired at the same time, but Lou had the advantage.

The Mexican knew he'd made a mistake, and as he rocked, with a bullet tearing his chest apart, he grinned, fleetingly and vainly. His pushed his gun back into his holster, half-turned in the direction of his fleeing partner, then folded neat and silent, before dropping to the ground.

Lou looked down at the man. In the Mexican's dying grimace, Lou saw the glitter of a gold tooth. He poked his toe at the body and murmured thoughtfully:

'Stupid kid. I was nothing to you. You should have stayed behind.'

To trail him nearly a hundred miles, just to pay off a bar-room grudge? A grudge of someone else's making, and to die for it? It didn't make sense. There had to be more to it than that. Still, Lou thought it unlikely Chimm would return, or the man who'd stood off and mentioned his name. Lou took a lingering look into the darkness. He listened for the slightest sound, but whoever'd been out there was way gone.

It was an instinct and the continuing silence that made Lou turn towards his horse. Instead of firing wildly, the young Mexican had thought of Lou's pursuit. The sorrel was dead with a thick, dark, rill across its neck. Its limbs twitched as it died, its head stretching along the blood-soaked ground.

Lou stared at the body of his dead mare in bitter anger, thought on how he should have taken both men, back in Cuidad Blanco. He'd have to make it on foot now, buy another horse at Red Bluff. It was a hell of a way toting a saddle and traps. The man called Tusk would be paying for it one day; the son-of-a-bitch who'd made mention of the Hollister family.

He pounded his Colt into the palm of his hand. One smack from the barrel was usually enough for a man, two would put down an ox if Lou put some meat behind it. From fifty feet, its .44 bullet could take away an arm. It was a bad mistake to have killed his horse, but an even bigger one to have left him with his gun.

He raised his arm high in the air, eased back the hammer and squeezed the trigger. The crack of the single shot would carry a vast distance. To the ears of those who had run, it proclaimed vengeance.

3

TEESIDE

Alford Cropper was emptying a rabbit trap. It was where a gully of the Pecos River broke flat and thin as it reached into the plain. Partly screened by the bole of a tupelo, he dropped a lank bundle of grey fur to the ground. He looked along the edge of water, pulled a heavy capote tight against the cold.

The house stood alongside the barn, a corral with a few fine horses and a rickety bunkhouse for itinerant cowboys. The house's adobe walls were three feet thick, kept it cool in summer, held the warmth in winter. The roof was holding up two feet of sod, and there were four windows inset with glass. The old man had provided his family with comforts, even through the years with little money and few cattle for market.

Alford's face was crumpled, the colour of dark soil. His eyes were all but black, and he had a stubble of silver hair. He turned to his eldest son, who was hefting a frayed sack. He listened patiently, as once again the young man vented his frustration.

'Another week, Father? Another month? How much longer do we allow Hollister's people to take from us? Until we have nothing, eh?'

'I don't know,' Alford answered wearily. 'But I know that to fight would bring suffering.'

'Yes, Father. As well as the shame it already brings us,' Barton responded bitterly. 'I am not a man who bears that easy.'

Alford's eyes wandered across his land. In the evening light it stretched as far as he could see. It was a good place, he thought, but for how much longer? And Barton was ready to risk it all.

Barton was still talking, his dark face burning with anger and frustration.

'These men of Tenbridge's, they're ridin' for Hollister,' he said, unable to control the shake in his voice. 'They treat us like the dirt you spend a lot of your life spittin' on.'

'That's right, Barton, they bring shame on us. But remember, once you start the fight you must carry on.' Alford tugged at the brim of his hat. 'You forget that Clew Hollister and I were friends at one time.'

'I'm not the one who's forgot, Pa. I'm not the one who's takin' food from the mouths of your children, or who hires gunmen to shoot at those who protest.'

The old man looked sharply at his son.

'That's not him, son. Not after all these years. But I'll go see him . . . talk about it. I know it's not *your* way, Barton, but *I'm* getting too old and tired for a fight.'

Barton was impatient and frustrated.

'Goin' to see Hollister won't help us. It's

17

Tenbridge who pulls the strings at Pasadera now.'

Alford watched Barton stride off towards his horse. He picked up the dead rabbit, and closed his eyes. He wanted to shut off the inevitable. Barton was proud, volatile, off to kick the rattler's nest. He'd fire up his brothers, and together they'd go up against the Pasadera crowd. That would be bad for all the Croppers.

Like most Texas cattlemen, Clewson Hollister had been dirt poor since the War between the States. Then, a short while ago, extra men were riding from his Pasadera ranch. It quickly became well known that these men were actually hired by the county sheriff, Tusk Tenbridge. In effect, Tenbridge was now running the spread. Now, Clewson Hollister was the owner of Pasadera in name only.

Texas was choking with such lawmen. They were appointed by the federal administration as peace-keepers, but Tusk Tenbridge was one of the few who worked too closely with crooked politicians and carpetbaggers.

The new hired hands eagerly thrust a Pasadera brand on everything that ate grass. Neighbouring stockmen had protested, only to end up flowering the desert as bleached bones.

Alford Cropper had suffered his losses too, and in his attempt to avoid further bloodshed had put a curfew on his headstrong boys. He was distressed because he couldn't understand the change. Before the war, the Hollisters had got on well enough with all their neighbours.

But the Hollister boys were gone. The eldest, Scorby, joined the Confederates and died in a Chesapeake swamp a year later. A day after the peace treaty was signed, and less than a mile outside of the Surrender Triangle, Tench was shot dead for his watch and boots. Lou, the young and uncontrollable one, never came home. Nobody knew what had happened to him.

Since then, old Clewson had turned inward, broken with sorrow at the loss of his boys. He could have got help from Alford to work the cattle, but he turned against him as he did against everyone else. The final blow came when some badly tied roof beams slipped from the side of a timber wagon. Clewson was helping to unload and both his feet were crushed. Consumed with bitterness, he'd mail-ordered a Bath chair and confined himself to it ever since. The only person prepared to offer comfort was Teresa, the niece of his dead wife.

The arrogant, Northern victors were plundering at will, but for Tusk Hollister to seize a man's ranch was over the line, even for that regime. It bothered Alford. He wondered why Clewson Hollister, whose belligerent allegiance had always been to the Southern states, appeared to have crumpled into defeat.

Alford Cropper had a gut feeling that it was going to get worse.

Two days later it did. Harlsey Cropper, the youngest of Alford's four boys was off hunting. He was splashing his pony through the bed of a shallow gully. He'd been day-dreaming, and he stopped sudden, his senses suddenly coming to. He reined in and stood in the stirrups to watch and listen. He knew the sounds and he could see what made them.

Along a stand of willow two riders crowded a bunch of long yearlings towards him. Harlsey heeled his pony forward. The riders were unmoved and apparently unconcerned at his approach. Harlsey pulled up, twisting the pony sideways across their path. His voice was sharply accusing as he opposed the men.

'Hey, what're you doin' with my pa's cattle?'

He was agitated and angry when he saw the brand on the calves. It had been a T, for the family brand of Teeside, but bad been crudely mutated. On its flank, every heifer now bore the recent crush of Clewson Hollister's Pasadera brand.

Harlsey knew about the men. The one with long, white hair was called Chimm. The other, not much older than Harlsey himself, was called Loomis Kraal. Loomis had a face like a small potato, and his hair curled greasily from under his stained woolsey hat. To Loomis Kraal, everything and anything was wretchedly amusing.

Kraal carried a border-draw pistol, and Harlsey could see Chimm's Winchester in a scabbard. To Harlsey's challenge, Chimm spat a glistening stream of juice over his shoulder.

'What's your interest, little cousin?' he asked offhandedly. He didn't expect any trouble from the boy, who appeared unarmed except for a small skinning-axe that he had tucked into his belt.

Loomis looked sideways at Harlsey and giggled. 'Why don't you tell him, baby red-coat?' He giggled again.

By now Harlsey was getting very nervous. Chimm and Kraal were notorious, even among Tenbridge's crowd. He was on his own, and he trembled with apprehension, but he owned a gun. It was a big old percussion revolver, which he'd had hidden ever since his father had imposed the curfew. He'd brought it out to shoot a few prairie chickens. It always fired when he wanted it to, provided it was kept clean and dry. But it was still rolled in an oilskin bag behind his saddle. He stared wide-eyed in defiance, saw the crude grin of Kraal, the pale, merciless eyes of Chimm.

'They're not your beef. You turn 'em loose, you hear. They're Teeside brand,' Harlsey croaked. As he spoke, he grappled behind him for the frame of the pistol.

'They *was* maybe. Now they're Pasadera,' Chimm rasped from deep in his throat.

As Harlsey dragged out the old pistol, Chimm shot him. The pony jerked away, and for a moment Harlsey continued his futile grab for the gun. He fumbled with his right hand, while his left clutched the thrashing reins of his pony.

As he fell sideways, his foot caught in his stirrup. Chimm watched impassively as the boy cried out, his body twisting and turning into the chill water of the stream. Harlsey's body trailed for a yard or two, until the stirrup released his foot. He shuddered, then for a short moment he lay still in the shallow gully, hardly breathing, with the side of his face resting on a smooth flat boulder. Then he died.

Chimm shoved his Winchester back into its scabbard.

'Courageous little tike, weren't he? What the hell did he think he was goin' to do with that heap o' scrap-iron, Loomis?'

'He would o' tried to blow your head off, Org,' Kraal replied. He giggled shrilly, and drooled spit on to his chin. He gaped at Harlsey's body. 'What we gonna do with him? Plant him with the others?'

Chimm gave a scornful grunt, and jerked back on the reins of his big grey.

'No, leave him be. Meat's scarce this time o' year. He won't go to waste.'

Scratching his head through his hat, Kraal stared after Chimm. He stayed to the rear, mumbling, waving the Teeside stock away from the gully, not bothering to look back.

4

THE SHERIFF OF TOYA BEND

It was early dark, and Lou Hollister was within a quarter mile of Toya Bend. It had been a long day's ride from Red Bluff, where he'd helped himself to trapper stew and an overpriced dun mare. He made a cautious advance on the broken ribbons of light, circling to the north, and lying close to the flat banks of the Pecos. The town didn't appear to have changed much since his youth. The river still looped around it, garnering strength in its journey towards an encounter with the Rio Grande.

He could see tallow-lamps in some windows of the buildings. He led the mare through short alleys, moving cautiously until he reached the main street. He stood amongst the debris of the shanties and listened, watched a group of scruffy, uniformed men cross the street.

So they were here too, he thought. Yankee soldiers

who'd never given up their killing ways. As with many
other towns in Texas, they'd made Toya Bend their
business centre. Some protected the carpetbaggers,
speculators and swindlers who came for the pickings.
Others lived off their wits, claiming everything for
themselves.

His horse faltered momentarily as a small boy
raced too close. Lou smiled coldly as the youngster
dragged a young javelina through the dust. It had a
long length of string, ring-tied through its nose, and
he had a friend running behind, beating its fat little
body with a broomstick. Lou shivered at the inane
cruelty and made encouraging noises as he walked
on.

Toya's Table entertained its small, regular clientele
of drinkers and drifters. Outside, there was a cowboy
rolling on the ground. He was tugging at his long
johns with one hand, and waving a small straw hat in
the other. His voice was breaking with emotion, as he
begged the forgiveness of a dishevelled, half-naked
woman.

The woman was wearing a shawl, loose woolly
drawers and short boots. She called out, '*sucio,
bastardo marrano,*' and staggered drunkenly up the
steps of the saloon.

A seasoned *vaquero* stood on the boardwalk talking
to himself. Every now and again he spat down at a
snuffling dog that crouched in the street.

Lou walked his horse up to the bar's hitching post,
and glanced along the line to a chestnut gelding,
standing quietly at the end. In front of him, a cowboy
sat in a deckchair with his legs propped on the low

railing. A slouch hat was pulled low across his face, but he was watching the street. As Lou stepped up beside him, he raised his head slightly.

'How do,' he said tentatively.

Lou nodded and looked back at the cowboy.

'If you've been sittin' there awhile, you'll know who rode in on the geldin'.'

There was a pause, and the cowboy let his feet drop to the ground.

'Well, I guess you recognize the brand.' The man pushed back his hat. 'Figgured you'd turn up one day, Hollister.'

Lou was startled. It was the second time his name had been used in near as many days.

'Yeah, well you got that right, fella,' he said. 'But I was askin' after who rides the geldin'.'

The cowboy answered slowly, and with a touch of cautiousness.

'Tusk Tenbridge.' He eyed Lou carefully. 'You'll find him inside. I wouldn't push him for a bill of sale though. He's with his friends.'

'What difference does that make?'

The cowboy gave a muffled snort. 'The difference *is*, he's the law. He's the sheriff of Cottonwood County, and those *friends* include businessmen and his deputy, as well as army.'

'I'll wait here,' said Lou. He suddenly looked more closely at the cowboy. 'If you know who I am, you'll know if there are any friends of *mine* hereabouts.'

This time the cowboy laughed. 'Most of 'em would be dead, I guess. Just supposin' you had any.'

The cowboy's response had no visible effect on Lou because for a moment he was deep in thought. Then he ticked a finger at the cowboy.

'You remind me o' Dooley Ricksen.'

'Yeah, me too, when I'm havin' a good day,' Ricksen said with a half-smile. 'An' if you know what's good for you, Lou Hollister, you'll ride on.'

Lou grinned back agreeably. 'Can't rightly do that just yet. Not until I've found out why this man's ridin' a horse with the Hollister brand across its rump.'

Ricksen shrugged, and eased himself up from his chair. He wore a buff jerkin and wear-faded denims, had a Le Mat's revolver tucked into a brass-buckled belt. He grinned back at Lou, and said derisively. 'Could be it's a legal horse trade. But then again . . . ?'

That was when the saloon doors flew open, and two men came out. One of them wore a faded trooper's uniform. As they stepped down into the street, their faces were shadowed by their hats. The army man carried an army-issue Colt, holstered high around his waist, and the tattered stripes of a corporal hung from his arm. For a moment the men stood talking and they didn't notice Lou moving along the boardwalk.

Tusk Tenbridge was a big man, in a long black coat. His broad hat was pulled tight over a shiny, hairless skull.

'Sheriff,' Lou said, his tone flat, but forceful. 'If you've a minute, there's somethin' botherin' me.'

Tenbridge was immediately wary. He peered up into the shadows of the saloon's low overhang.

'Do I know you, mister?' His practised cunning sensed danger, and he moved sideways away from his colleague, ready to outflank Lou. 'Who the hell are you?' He shifted his eyes to Dooley Ricksen.

Lou chilled at the sound of Tusk Tenbridge's low voice.

'It's Lou Hollister,' Ricksen cut in, to Tenbridge's fierce question. 'Clewson's boy. He's come back.'

Either on purpose or out of caution, the sheriff's aide hadn't moved away, and Tenbridge himself wasn't alarmed at Lou's confrontation. The big man spoke rudely.

'Seems I've heard the name. Whoever you are, boy, you start trouble here an' you won't live to finish it. This corporal o' mine don't look much, but he'll shoot ya where ya stand if he has to.' Tenbridge had seen the surreptitious movement of Lou's hand. He was doing Lou's thinking for him.

Lou had been considering the possibility of a fight when Ricksen moved in behind him. He knew that even with the advantage of two, or three to one, Tenbridge couldn't be that sure, unless he'd a big advantage. And Tenbridge knew it too. He'd be the first to die, if Lou pulled the Colt.

The brief impasse was broken when Dooley Ricksen pushed in with his sharp warning.

'Don't do it, Lou. I can't miss from where I'm standin'.'

Dooley was Tenbridge's advantage, and he was holding the grapeshot revolver. A small smile broke across his face.

'Sorry, Lou, you should o' thought it out.'

'You'd never have tried that facin' me, Dooley,' Lou snapped at him.

Ricksen's smile vanished, and his manner turned prickly.

'Don't get too smart, Lou. You're gonna learn the Hollisters ain't throwin' their weight around Cottonwood County any more.'

Tenbridge took off his sweat-stained hat and swiped his hand across the top of his head.

'Up to this moment, Dooley, I been wonderin' if you knew which way the wind was blowin'.' Then he winked meanly at Lou. He turned to the man with corporal's stripes. 'Take his gun, Mel.'

The man stepped forward and snatched at Lou's Colt.

'What now, Tusk? he asked. The few words carried a whiff of excitement. 'Take him out a-ways?'

Tenbridge tutted and pursed his lips at the suggestion. 'And introduce him to your "necktie friends"? No, Mel. We got to let Mr Hollister see there's a law to uphold.'

Lou wanted to turn on Dooley Rickssen, but he kept his eyes locked on Tenbridge, who was nodding at Mel.

'Take him to the jail. Tell Wishbone to lock him up. As far as I'm concerned he's a no-good drifter, an' I'm arrestin' him on suspicion o' murder.'

Mel struck the frame of the big Colt against Lou's spine.

'You heard the sheriff, an' you know which way we're headed. Get goin'.'

Lou looked calmly at Tenbridge. 'What about my horse?'

'Someone'll take it down to the livery stable. Belongs to you does it, the mare?'

'You're the one that's ridin' a steal horse, Sheriff.'

Tenbridge slapped his hat against his leg. 'I'll get Mel to push a bit through that puss o' yours, Hollister,' he rasped humourlessly.

5

THE SET-UP

Clewson Hollister sat stony-faced in his wheeled chair. Bony hands were clenched on the plaid rug that stretched tight across his knees. His hair was thin and unkempt, and wiry brows clutched the tops of his sunken eyes as he scowled at the girl.

Through a window, Teresa was watching the men in the ranch enclosure. She turned and spoke to the old man, her voice flat and cheerless.

'What is it you see in those men that I can't? Why do you have them around, Clewson?'

'I don't see anythin' in 'em, 'cause from here I can't,' he said harshly. 'They have the advantage of not bein' overseen, in case you hadn't noticed.'

Teresa bit her lip. Her positioning was bad. She was caught between Clewson and the cause of all he'd lost and she moved away from the window.

Clewson looked up at her, then down at his hands. 'They're garbage and they're trouble. But what can I do, Tess?'

Teresa was his dead wife's niece, and she'd looked after him since his accident. She was small, and had coal black hair, wore only homespuns because there wasn't much reason for anything better.

'I don't know,' she said kindly, and suddenly smiled. 'I was going to tell you. One of them put the make on me, the other day.'

Clewson glared and raised his fists. 'Put the make on? Who are you talkin' about?' He made a grab for his stick, and cracked it against the side of his chair.

The intensity made Tess start. 'It's all right. It wasn't much more than he's tried since I arrived here. I can handle him. If I can't, I'll call you for help.'

Clewson's frustrated misery welled up. 'I can't even look after you properly, can I?'

Teresa moved towards Clewson.

'I'm supposed to be looking out for *you*, remember?' she told him. 'The man was herding me some, that's all.' She kneeled on the floor beside him and put her hands over his. 'Don't fear for me, Clew. Just tell me what they're really doing here.'

Clewson sat for a few moments before he spoke. He was obviously suffering from remorse.

'It was after the boys had gone. Tenbridge came to see me. He offered to help, and I made a deal with him. I had to try and keep the ranch, Tess.'

Teresa could see the anguish as the old man carried on:

'It was so easy for him, an' I didn't see it. He was goin' to arrange for the cattle to be driven north. There's fat money for beef at Fort Sumner.'

Teresa looked at him, not understanding. 'More money than we can make down here, yes. But what happened, Clew?' She watched as Clewson's jaw trembled.

'He took the money. He still does. It was a good deal for him. The worst for me. We get nothing except . . .' Clewson's words trailed off.

Teresa gently broke into his despair. 'So that's what they've been doing. Driving the stock out of State, then they're railroaded back into Texas?'

'Now you know, Tess. Tenbridge's been suckin' the blood out of the ranch. He'll be moving on the house next.' Fearing the loss of everything, Hollister stared bleakly around the room. As if he'd forgotten Tess, he stumbled on: 'If I had the boys . . . but on my own . . . a washed-up cripple . . . .'

Teresa went back to look out of the window.

'Don't let go yet, Clew. There'll be a way out.' She turned to face him. 'Why not get someone else to take a herd to Cuidad Blanco?'

'Someone else,' he snarled. 'There's no *someone* else. They're all as bad as each other. Even them long-time, neighbourly Croppers have been stringing my heifers across to Sweetwater . . . Abilene, even.'

'You've no proof of that Clew. Your mind's been poisoned,' Teresa objected.

Since Tench, his second son, had been killed, Clewson had suffered these dark bouts. Teresa wondered whether she herself was getting beyond his regard and trust.

'Why don't you ask Dooley Ricksen? He's honest, isn't he?'

'Dooley Ricksen? I know you mean well, gal, but no. There's no way out. I'm finished.'

Teresa rubbed her hands across her face, smearing tears. There wasn't much point in discussing or encouraging. She'd have to come up with something herself. There was no doubting Tusk Tenbridge's duplicity, but she wasn't sure how far Clewson's mind had deteriorated. She wouldn't quit on him though, regardless of any danger to herself. They could still fight.

6

DOOLEY RICKSEN

It was approaching full dark as Tusk Tenbridge watched his deputy push Lou Hollister down the street.

'That'll close him up a bit,' he said, his heavy body rolling with satisfaction. He narrowed his eyes at Dooley Ricksen. 'Maybe I did have you pegged out wrong, Dooley. I was thinkin' you an' Hollister were sometime pals.'

Ricksen shrugged. 'I knew him, but not close. I had an understandin' with his brother. They were just huckster schemes, though.'

Tenbridge clapped a big hand on Ricksen's shoulder.

'You know there's work for a man like you, Dooley,' he said. 'There's money to be made, and I'm thinkin' favourably on it.'

They stood outside the saloon until they were joined by Dowse Bittleman, a lumber merchant, and Chester Bumpass, the small, pasty-faced man who owned the hardware store. Bumpass was unsteady on his feet because he'd been drinking all evening.

'I do so like the dark, gentlemen,' he said thickly. 'Nothing seems quite as bad.'

Tenbridge shot a glance at Bittleman, who simply shrugged his shoulders.

Bumpass continued: 'Well, gentlemen, we can't stand around here all night. Join me for supper.'

Again, Tenbridge looked questioningly at Bittleman. Bumpass, said more directly:

'I'll guarantee my supper's an improvement on the swill we've been paying for in there. If you'll just follow me,' he said, rolling his eyes at the prospect.

'Yeah, thanks Chester,' Tenbridge said. 'The town seems peaceable enough. An' as I'm the only one who's unrestricted in the trouble they can cause round here . . .' He laughed significantly at his observation.

The three men walked across the street. Dooley Ricksen was uncertain behind them, but Tenbridge turned and waved him forward.

Lamps were burning in Bumpass's store, and an assistant edged past them as they pushed in. Bumpass ignored him, apart from accepting a large bunch of keys as they passed in the doorway. He led the men to the back of the store, through stacked flour bags and barrels. He stumbled against the end of his packed counter, before fumbling a key into the door of his storeroom and office.

'Come in, gentlemen. It's not only hammers and nails that I stock,' he said genially.

The room was a clutter of frontier commodities.

Everything from canned milk and horehound candy to shovels and catch ropes. In the corner were two chairs and a davenport. Bumpass eased himself down full-length, and pointed to a small cupboard above his head.

'Please help yourselves, gentlemen. I fear the evening has had the better of me.' He folded his plump fingers across his chest, and within moments he was snoring, loud and raucous.

Tusk Tenbridge inspected the bottle he took down from Bumpass's cupboard.

'Well, he was right about the mark of his whiskey. Double-rectified, old corn.'

Dooley Ricksen stood uncomfortably and hoped it was deceiving Tenbridge. He wondered why the sheriff had wanted him along, but he accepted his share of the good whiskey.

'He won't be hearin' much for a while,' Tenbridge said, looking down at Bumpass. He sat heavily in one of the chairs, and nodded for Ricksen to sit facing him at the table. Bittleman remained standing, with a knowing smirk across his face.

Tenbridge held up his glass. 'Welcome, Dooley. But I'm thinkin' maybe there's a question of – er – loyalty,' he suggested, looking cagily at Ricksen.

'I can be loyal. Do you want somethin' of me?' Ricksen asked suspiciously.

'Well, yeah, there *is* somethin', Dooley,' Tenbridge replied, as he topped up their glasses. The sheriff drew a short-barrelled, single-action revolver that he'd been carrying in his frock-coat. He placed it in front of Ricksen, and smiled.

'It's about that man, Hollister. We can do without him turnin' up here an' now. Ain't that a fact, Dooley?'

Ricksen put his glass on the table, and stared at the gun.

'You want him got rid of? Is that the somethin' you're talkin' about?' He glanced at Bittleman, looking and sounding suitably shocked.

Tenbridge chortled, and shook his head slowly. 'We're lookin' for someone to turn him round, that's all. I *was* put here as an officer of the law, remember.'

Bumpass snored contentedly. There wasn't much doubt of his involvement in any profitable scheming, but he was well out of the setting up.

The sheriff thumbed the cylinder from the pistol. He looked up as he ejected each charge.

'Now listen up, Dooley. Here's what we'd like you to do.'

Carefully leaving the gun's percussion caps in position, his expression became more serious as he explained. Bittleman took advantage of the corn whiskey, as Dooley Ricksen's task became clearer.

7

DEADWOOD

The mud-faced walls gleamed from the light of the lamp that hung outside the door of Lou's cell. He looked around him gloomily at the litter-bed against one wall, the barred window and the dirt-can. The overpowering whiff stung his eyes and the back of his throat.

The night they'd tried to shoot Lou up at his night camp, it had been Tusk Tenbridge who had stayed back. It was Tenbridge who had mentioned the Hollister name. That was why they'd dogged him all the way from Cuidad Blanco. Tenbridge must have been there, with Chimm. But they'd also been on the return to Toya Bend. Lou's stars were crossed all right. He'd been guilty of a murder before he pulled up outside Toya's Table.

He couldn't understand Tenbridge indicting him for killing Herido, the young Mexican. It had been outside the Texas border, but it seemed that Tenbridge was law in more than Toya Bend. It was

Tenbridge's *own* law, wherever it stretched, and whatever he said it was. The sheriff wasn't thinking of a trial. His deputy, Mel Pawkson certainly wasn't. He'd be for the nearest tree, and a summary hanging. It was probably why Cottonwood County was so called, Lou thought in bleak humour.

Facing the window, he hunched down with his back against the cell door. Yeah, that would be it, he thought. Tenbridge was on the hop because Lou's last name was Hollister, not because he'd killed Herido, or of his run-in with Chimm.

Organ Chimm must have recognized his name; recalled it from the prison ship that went north to Vicksburg and the federal stockade. As an able-bodied captive, Lou's name would have been on a roster, and Chimm had seen it, made the link with Pasadera. He couldn't have been certain, though, and whatever was going on now, Tenbridge wanted Lou out of the way, just in case there was a family connection. It had to be something to do with his father and the ranch. Tenbridge was even riding a horse with an Pasadera brand. Lou's heart thumped with helpless anxiety. He knew there was something badly wrong.

Since he'd ridden off to join the army there'd been no contact between Lou and his father, or his brothers. Maybe they'd known of his capture, but no message or letter ever came through. And he hadn't written home; he'd been too ashamed of the humiliation of Natchez. Cuidad Blanco had confirmed that the in-between years hadn't changed much.

Lou had to stop his mind racing and turn his

thoughts to something more practical. He'd been coming home anyway, and meeting Chimm wasn't bad luck or timing, it was fate.

He unbent from his crouched position, and stepped over to the window. The sky was turning from deep grey to black, but by pushing the side of his face hard against the bars, he could just see where the alley bent around the jail. At the corner, in the yellow light of an open doorway, there was an old man thumbing a Jew's-harp. Lou squinted to see the other way, but that end of the alley was too dark to reveal anything. It was a plaintive tune and he'd heard it before, placed it somewhere along the Mississippi riverbank.

Lou stopped the memory as a nosing rat scuttled across the dirt floor. He shuddered, then backed off from the window. The jail was set well back from the main street. It was gripped in the pungency of animal fur, stable dust and canhouse swill, and it caused his stomach to churn.

He knew the geography well enough. There were corrals behind the livery barn, and a run of stock-sheds; then open land, straight to the rim of the Edwards Plateau. He'd have to come up with something.

He stared at the rickety frame of the litter. In the Vicksburg pen, he'd found a rusty metal bracket. He'd bound one end and sharpened the other on a stone to fashion a mean weapon. Confused, fleeting memories of a Yankee guard returned, and Lou kicked recklesly and angrily at the litter, as he thought back.

Dooley Ricksen. What was his problem? He'd talked real nice. Then he'd pulled that grapeshot revolver and offered Lou to the sheriff. Lou's face twisted into a scowl. Perhaps the deception was worthy of some admiration, but if Lou got hold of him . . . .

He lay, troubled and weary on the broken litter. Why had Dooley done that? They'd got along well enough growing up, even though Dooley had been a better friend of his brother, Tench. Now it had all changed, and Dooley Ricksen was running with the other side.

An hour later a sound woke him. His nerves tightened when across the bars of the small window a face appeared. It was darkly silhouetted against the black sky. His muscles seized with fear as reality snapped him from the remnants of a weary sleep. Tenbridge had ordered him to be thrown in jail, but had he changed his mind? Had he sent someone from the 'necktie party' he'd mentioned?

Lou pushed himself up and away from the litter. He moved to the far wall, standing still and helpless as the low whispers reached into the cell.

'Lou, you in there? Come over here.' It was the voice of Dooley Ricksen.

Lou shivered involuntarily from the icy sweat that ran between his shoulder blades. If Ricksen meant to shoot him, there wasn't a lot he could do about it.

'Found another safe place, Ricksen? All I've got is a piss-pot, this time,' he said derisively, thinking he'd die toughing it out.

'Listen up Hollister. I don't have much time. Take this,' Ricksen retorted.

Lou stared as Ricksen thrust his hand through the window bars. He was holding a short-barrelled revolver. Lou didn't move. If he went forward, Ricksen could turn the gun and shoot him. From that close up he wouldn't miss, even in the dark.

'Didn't figure on me bein' in here, and still alive, did you Ricksen?' he said, his nerves still jumping.

'For Chrissake, Lou, just listen. You're in bad trouble, and not thinkin' straight.' He moved, and Lou could see the thinnest of lamplight across his face. Lou sidled further into the corner of the cell as Ricksen continued: 'Just think for a second. You'd be layin' in a pine box right now, if it hadn't been for me. You seriously think you could have shot down the sheriff an' his deputy?'

'You should have given me the chance to find out, Ricksen. What was my life to you?'

'I don't have time to argue with you, Lou. Take the gun an' do what I say, an' maybe you'll get out of here alive. It's up to you.'

Lou stayed where he was.

'Keep talkin',' he said. 'I can't do much else but listen.'

'It's a deadwood situation from Tenbridge. The gun's primed, but not loaded. Wishbone checks you out, before he turns in. When he does . . . well, the rest's up to you.'

'Yeah, and what if old Wishbone knows about it? Goodnight by his shotgun?'

'He aint goin' to shoot. You're *supposed* to get out.'

'When *does* he shoot me then?'

'He doesn't, for Chrissakes. You'll run straight into a couple o' so-called deputies. *They'll* shoot you.'

'Is that the best you can come up with, Ricksen?'

'Take the gun, Lou. Have a look. I've reloaded it. I can't stay around here any longer.'

Lou tried quickly to sort it out. If he could get his hands on the gun, and it *was* loaded and primed, he'd have nothing to lose; unless there was something he hadn't thought on. But that was the chance he'd have to take.

'Leave it on the ledge,' he said, a shade uneasily. He didn't know whether it was a short cut to the grave patch, but at least he'd have a gun.

He watched closely as Ricksen placed the gun between the bars, across the thick ledge. He decided he'd give one more person one more chance.

'I'll see how it goes. Maybe leave the thankin' for later on,' he said, quiet and thoughful.

'Don't forget them two deputies. I'll have the horses out beyond the corrals,' Ricksen told him. 'We'll both be kickin' out o' this town,' he said, dropping back to the alley.

8

FLIGHT

Lou left it ten minutes before he made a move for the gun. He checked it, and sure enough, it was in firing order. He sat on the floor, his head in his hands. There was a lot happening, and he didn't have the measure of any of it. Even if Dooley Ricksen was on the level, his allegiance to Lou was a shaky one. Either side of the cell wall, Lou's immediate future was grim.

Ricksen had said that Tenbridge's deputies would 'take him' when he walked from the jail. He held a loaded gun now, but the killers would have a big advantage. He'd have to change the rules.

The jailer checked on him before midnight, but Lou didn't attempt his breakout. It was a way of testing Ricksen's stance. Lou was still worried about the jailer, and after he'd gone, he lay awake for nearly four hours. No one visited the jail, and Lou decided that the man hadn't been privy to Tenbridge's arrangement. He'd make his move at first light;

make the deputies wait for their treacherous work. He'd give himself the edge of surprise, and a couple of hours' faltering rest.

It was approaching five when Lou heard Wishbone stomping around in the front office of the jail. There was the drift of coffee, and his uneasy stomach could look forward to corn bread, and maybe something in a bowl.

He'd force himself to be patient, get some sustenance, before he made his move. He was standing with his hands against the bars when old Wishbone brought through the early meal.

'With only me to look after, you must get real bored,' Lou said. 'What do you do all day?'

Wishbone pushed through the coffee and meagre food. 'Beat me at checkers . . . sometimes. What's it to you?' he added curtly.

'Nothin'. I just wondered. Envious I guess.'

The old jailer looked into the cell. 'What's yer bed doin' stood up over there?'

Lou looked at the litter he'd propped against the wall beside the window. 'It's broken. Anyway, it gives me more room. I don't take to confined spaces.'

'Well, put it back. I don't like it there,' Wishbone said. 'Put it back where it should be, else I won't take out yer dirt-pail.'

'Yessir. I'll see to it when I've finished my breakfast.' Lou responded quietly, as Wishbone wandered back to the office.

He made short work of the food, then tucked Ricksen's gun into the front of his pants. He pulled the litter from the wall, and slammed it hard down on to the floor. He yelled loudly, then quickly wedged himself beneath the shattered slats.

Within moments Wishbone was peering through the bars.

'What the Sam Hill you done, boy? Can you hear me, Hollister?' He hurried back for the keys to the cell, muttering with the rub of genuine concern.

Lou slid the gun between his chest and the underside of the litter, closed his eyes and waited for Wishbone.

Wishbone was gibbering as he twisted the cell keys and pushed open the door. He stooped towards Lou who was lying still and silent beneath the litter.

'You ain't killed yerself, have you, boy?' he quavered.

'No,' Lou said, smiling broadly up into the old man's worried face. He eased out the gun, and aimed it at Wishbone's stomach. 'Pull this crate off me.'

Wishbone seemed more relieved than frightened, as he eased the litter clear of Lou.

'You had me real worried there for a while.'

Lou got to his feet, and nodded. 'Thanks. Where's your shotgun?'

'I didn't think I'd need it,' Wishbone said. 'It's in the gun rack. Why? You ain't gonna shoot me, are yer, boy? I done you no harm.'

'I know you haven't, and I ain't gonna shoot you. Just keep quiet.'

Wishbone held up his shaking hands. 'I will. I been doin' that for longer'n I can remember.'

Lou stared at him for a few seconds. 'Good. I'm

not even goin' to lock you up. But you'll be stayin' here, an' you won't even make the sound of a bum calf. Stay here, until the sheriff arrives.'

Lou stood outside the cell and looked towards the office. 'Have you got my gun out there?'

Wishbone just pointed.

Lou narrowed his eyes. 'Remember. If you do anythin' before then, I'll come back and do some-thin' *real* bad to that old body o' yours.'

Knowing the jailer was too frightened to move, Lou walked to the office. A steaming mug of coffee stood on Wishbone's well-used checker board, and the door of the gun rack sagged open above a desk. He grunted when he caught sight of his own gun lying under a sheaf of Wanted posters. He removed the cylinder from Ricksen's gun, and tossed the frame on to the desk. He checked the cylinder and caps of his Colt, and gripped the butt reassuringly. With his left hand he reached into the rack and took Wishbone's shotgun.

His muscles were tense, and he was sweating a little, as he edged out of the jail. He took a couple of deep breaths, and looked uneasily around him. He backed into the alley that sided the jail, and paused again to listen. There was no yelling, and nobody shot at him; only a rooster crowed in the distance.

Carrying two guns, he sidled towards the rear of the jail. He stopped at the end of the alley, and compassed the ground ahead. He saw a cluster of sheds to his left and, ahead of him, the corral, which held a lone horse. Beyond that, the open range, crushed and colourless, under the flat, early light.

He moved into the lee of the sheds. The horse was fractious, and he watched as it raised its head, flick-eared, towards the street side of the corral, the side nearest the jail. Lou leaned the shotgun carefully against the wall of the shed, and stepped out.

Outlined against the cold glow from the east, he'd seen the men he wanted. They were close together, talking quietly, paid to be waiting. There was no mistaking their identity, both were wearing army-issue pants, and carrying sidearms.

'You two,' he called. 'Waitin' for me?'

The two deputies looked at each other in sudden alarm. One of them recovered quickly and glared towards Lou.

'You took your time, mister,' he barked. 'We been numbin' ourselves out here.'

The smaller of the two idled sideways, laughing. He nodded at the gun in Lou's hand.

'How you playin' it, Hollister? You gonna throw that thing at us first, or after you've pulled the trigger?'

Lou gave a genuine smile. He could hardly believe it.

'No, you've got it all wrong. Take a close look at the gun.' His head scarcely moved in the direction of his hand. 'Not quite what you were expectin', you murderin' trash. This is my big ol' Colt. I returned it to me, on the way out.'

The deputies' faces flicked back and forth, between the gun and Lou's face. They paled, and their bodies tensed. They wanted to look at each other, but didn't dare take their eyes off Lou.

Lou almost hissed at them. 'Now, how do *you* want to play it?'

His gut hardened, and he slowly lowered the big Colt to his side. The ruthless bullies would have shot him dead, unarmed and defenceless. He waited for a sign of movement, but it wasn't possible to keep his concentration on both; they were too far spread.

That was what they were relying on. There was a thin, taunting sneer from the man on the left, but Lou didn't flinch. There was no other way now, and he knew it would be the small one who'd shoot first.

The irked horse slammed its hoofs into the poles of the low corral, and Lou knew it was the moment. He caught the small one grabbing for his holster.

Before the barrel had cleared leather, Lou had thumbed back the hammer of his Colt. The man jerked back as the bullet struck him in the the chest. He was lifted up on his toes, as if trying to appear taller, then he pitched forward, slamming into the hard-packed dirt. Lou watched as the man's hand dragged again at his gun, but it was over, and the body finally caved in. He stepped forward to the life-less deputy. He looked at the dead face, then back at the second man who was standing rooted to the spot.

He gaped with foreboding at Lou. 'Not me mister. I'm not sworn in, never was. I'm just wearin' the badge. It don't mean nothin'.'

'It should. It's just cost you your life.' Lou pulled back the hammer for the second time.

The man had to make a try to live, and he made a futile grab for his own Colt. Lou waited for him to level the gun, and he shook his head as the doomed man palmed the hammer with his other hand. Lou's bullet caught him in the left shoulder, spinning him round with the impact. Clutching his gun in both hands, the man managed to fire one shot that ploughed into the ground between his buckling legs. Lou fired again, and the man crashed back against the corral. He hung there for several seconds, then fell, throwing his gun out ahead of him.

Lou pushed the Colt beneath his coat.

'Don't know how much Tenbridge's paid you men for this, but it really weren't near enough,' he muttered.

In the shadows behind him there was movement. Two or three people had already appeared, and Lou looked at their unresponsive faces, as if encouraging a reprisal, but they didn't seem to know what to do, or appear to care. As he moved off, a mangy grey dog with a dead chicken in its mouth sprang from the corral. Lou looked directly into the spiteful yellow eyes, and instinctively moved his hand back to his Colt. Then, from beyond the stock-sheds, a voice yelled, short and urgent.

'Don't, Lou. Get over here.'

The man was wearing ill-fitting clothes and a slouch hat. He led a Pasadera horse, the chestnut gelding Lou had seen tied outside Toya's Table. Lou took the reins and climbed eagerly into the saddle.

'You're full of surprises, Dooley,' he said, as he swung the horse around. 'We'll ride north, while you make good the explainin'.'

9

THE SHORT STORY

They took to the plain, scattering winter rabbit and quail from their mesquite hiding-places. They maintained an easy pace, and kept to the course of the Pecos as it wound up to the foothills. Every hour they allowed the horses a drink where the water shallowed. They rode until they were fifty miles northeast of Toya Bend. The land threw deep, orange light into their faces, and the distant Sacramentos stood black and dark against the disappearing sun.

They stopped and stood alone, watched the misty breath of their own heavy breathing. The muscles of Lou's gelding quivered, its coat glistening in the darkness as it pawed the earth in anticipation of late clover. Dooley Ricksen had brought supplies, and shortly the men feasted off hot beans, onions, eggs and corn bread.

An hour later Lou made himself easy, with his back firmly bolstered in the curve of his saddle. He drew a slicker and blanket around him, laid his head back, and looked directly up into the inky-blue darkness.

'Listen to me, Dooley Ricksen,' he said. 'In the last few days, I've had to shoot at half a dozen men. Three of them are dead. Now you tell me why.'

'You've been gone a long time, Lou, and what's happened ain't good. An' in case you're still wonderin', Tenbridge would have had those deputies put bullets in *me*. I knew too much an' I owe you for that.'

'That's as maybe, Dooley. I want to know the rest.'

Dooley tossed the dregs of his coffee into the fire. 'I'll give you the rest, Lou, but you ain't gonna like it.' He cleared his throat. 'Your brother, Scorby, was killed at Chickamauga. Tench made it through safely, but . . .' Dooley's voice faltered. 'Then he met up with a group of Tenbridge's men.'

A short silence followed before Lou spoke.

'What happened, Dooley?'

'It was only a mile from where old Lee furled his flag. They'd been drinkin' . . . reckoned that Tench's boots an' watch was stole from the body of a Union officer. Tench could have told 'em they belonged to his pa . . . your pa. If he'd gone for his gun, it would only have been to scare 'em off. He ought to have had more sense. One of 'em shot him out o' the saddle.'

'How do you know all this?' Lou quickly wanted to know.

'Word got round. This country ain't always *so* big. Loomis Kraal was shootin' his mouth off. Said he rode away with Tench's horse. You remember Domus Kraal, over at Gander Creek? Loomis is his eldest.'

'Yeah, I remember 'em. Loomis was no more'n a kid. An ugly peewee from what I remember. Was it him shot Tench?'

'No, that was Chimm. Organ Chimm.'

'Chimm?' Lou repeated. 'What's he look like?'

'Tall, long white hair, mangy. You know him?'

'We've met, but I never knew his name,' Lou said thoughtfully.

He told Dooley about the confrontation at Cuidad Blanco, and about Chimm and the Mexican coming at him, later.

'Chimm was a jailer on a US prison ship. It was Tenbridge though, who mentioned my name. I still don't know what the hell he was talking about, Dooley. I hope you're goin' tell me?'

Dooley was suddenly surprised and curious.

'You were at Vicksburg? That was a prisoner o' war camp. How'd you get yourself there?'

'It's a long story. Not for the tellin' now.'

'Jeez, you know how to light the fuse o' trouble, Lou. The Mex you killed was Herido Ochenta. He was almost real people to Chimm.'

Lou was unmoved. He stared at the last of the fire's embers as they split and sparked.

'Why was Tusk Tenbridge ridin' the Pasadera horse, Dooley? You never did answer me that.'

Dooley was uneasy, and his reply was hesitant.

'It seems like he's some influence on your old man . . . got him in his clutches . . . that's what some are sayin', Lou. Even got his eye on the girl, apparently.'

'What girl?' Lou asked.

Dooley thought for a second. 'A bit after your

time,' he said. 'Teresa's her name. Her mother brought her all the way from somewhere in Georgia. They were refugees. I think Mrs Beecroft was your ma's sister.'

Lou's own mother had been dead a long time, but he thought he remembered the name of her sister: Mrs Beecroft was Lou's aunt. The girl meant nothing to him, but he was stunned at what Dooley had to say about his father, and that Tenbridge had a hold over him. What could have happened? Clewson Hollister always took 'point', and never kowtowed to anyone.

'There's something very wrong, Dooley.' Lou felt the agitation of guilt creeping through him.

'Yeah. He certainly hit a dry lode, Lou. He was left with Teresa when Mrs Beecroft was taken with a bad fever. Maybe that was all right though; she's looked after him since. He calls her Tess. She was there when the wood fell on him. He ain't done much since.'

Lou pulled his Stetson over his face. For all his toughness, his jaw twitched at the thought of knowing they'd suffered by his not being there. After Vicksburg, he should have come home. He hadn't known of his dead brothers, or his father's accident, but he could still give himself a hard time over it.

'Tusk Tenbridge,' he said slowly. 'Where does he come from?'

'Don't know. Up north somewhere. He was put into Toya Bend by the administrators.'

'And for a cherry, he moved in on Pasadera,' Lou snapped bitterly.

'I think so, Lou. Your old man ain't up to opposin'

54

him. Not the way he is now. All that happened bent his mind. He don't trust nobody.'

'Did he trust Tenbridge?'

'At the beginnin' maybe. I don't rightly know. He don't get out, I know that much. He's only got Tess.' Dooley stopped for a moment. 'That's the problem Tenbridge's got with you, Lou. After all this time . . . just turnin' up.'

Lou lay very still. The silence was affecting, but Dooley decided to carry on.

'Tenbridge's men are ridin' roughshod across the range. They're stickin' their own brand on all live-stock. Everyone's sufferin'. There's no one to stop 'em, Lou. Maybe if . . .'

Recognizing the impact of his telling, Dooley went quiet. But after a few minutes of intense silence, he asked tentatively, 'What you gonna do, Lou?'

'For starters, get me some sleep.'

In the early morning, they woke to the fresh, biting cold. Lou's horse was standing near watching him, its head bathed in a cloud of spiralling steam. Lou cantered it around the withered remains of the camp-fire to stir their circulations and taut muscles.

Dooley had found branchwood, so they could make hot coffee. He looked deliberately at Lou.

'You're goin' to Pasadera, aren't you?'

Lou nodded. 'Yeah, I am. As far as I know, the ranch still belongs to the Hollister family, and that includes *me*. It's about time I did somethin' about it.'

'You'll need help, Lou. Guess I'll tag along.'

Lou grinned wryly. 'This ain't anythin' to do with

you, Dooley, an' I'm real obliged. But . . .'

Dooley shook his head. 'No, Lou, I'm comin' with you. Lookin' out for your old man's the same as lookin' out for all of us. Why don't we just pack up and get goin'?'

It was an hour past daybreak when the two men rode towards Pasadera ranch.

10

CHIMM'S POSSE

It was mid-morning, and the thin, heatless sun fell through the raggedy blinds of the sheriff's office in Toya Bend.

Tusk Tenbridge's smugness had deserted him, and he slammed his fist on the desk top. He was bloated with anger as he stared across the table.

'How the hell'd they get away?' he fumed.

Herran Stiles was a Northerner; took turn as top hand when Organ Chimm was away. He wore a mix of old army. His face was covered with short, stickly hair, and his eyes squeezed with tension.

'Dooley Ricksen,' he said rapidly. 'He took your horse from the livery. No one to do much about it, at that hour. Must o' been real late, or real early.'

Tenbridge swore slowly, with every sacrilegious phrase he could think of. It helped bring his temper under control. 'I should o' known.' There was a dash of a crooked smile across his face.

'He suckered me.'

Stiles squinted at Tenbridge. He wanted activity, but he said nothing.

Tenbridge looked back at him, hard and thoughtful. 'Get someone you can trust. Send 'em to Pasadera. Tell Domus Kraal to stay awake. Hollister's likely to try and get to his pa.'

Stiles was ready and eager. 'Done. What about me?'

'Find me another horse, goddammit. We'll get out to the herd. An' tell 'em to take guns. They'll be needed.'

Stiles left the office quickly and Tenbridge gripped the ends of his desk. Ricksen taking his horse was going to be something he'd regret. It wouldn't be long before an ironic snigger spread around the town. He shivered and his skin was already goosed, as he pulled himself from his chair.

Lou Hollister was worse news; he'd killed two more men. Nothing good had happened since Cuidad Blanco. He remembered the night they'd shot up Hollister's camp. He could have died out there himself, instead of Herido Ochenta. Tenbridge shuddered, like someone who'd just had their grave walked over.

He thought how close he'd been – still was – to moving in on Pasadera. He'd got it all worked out. Poor old Clewson Hollister was sliding away, with his mind in a mess. And then there was Teresa. He drew breath at the thought of the girl. It was looking like a ready-made, a winner, but now with the arrival of Lou Hollister, none of it was such a sure bet.

He heard loud talking, and horses snorting in the

street. He grabbed a Winchester and took a box of ammunition from his desk drawer. Lou Hollister was on a loose lead, but from now on there was no more slack in Tusk Tenbridge's rope.

Hooper Crewle's chuckwagon was wedged in a stand of alder. A twist of smoke climbed from the fire, where he was preparing the usual sowbelly, beans and biscuits. Smells of the cooking drifted to Tusk Tenbridge and his men, where they watched from the top of a low rise.

Tenbridge eyed the rope corral that held the small remuda of cow- and pack-ponies. Clustered in hundreds of small groups, the herd had started to mill across its bed ground.

This was the herd set to be driven to the Cuidad Blanco railhead. Most were Pasadera, but it was a stock mix. The cowboys hadn't been too careful about brand marks during their rounding-up. The herd was close to a thousand head, Tenbridge figured.

'Let's get down there,' he called.

Followed by Herran Stiles, Brewster Zube, and Walter Henn, he rode down towards the camp.

Crewle was a stove-up wrangler, with arthritis and bent legs that had never healed straight from multiple breakings. He wore a canvas bag apron and an irked expression. He gestured at the big pot hanging from the tailgate.

'There's an inch of the first coffee. Its crusty but still warm. If you're lookin' for food, it ain't ready yet.'

Tenbridge dismounted and tipped some stewed coffee into a tin mug. He stared at the contents, then at Crewle.

'Can't see Chimm? Where is he?'

'Checkin' the herd, I guess. He don't always tell me his plans,' was the cook's sour response.

'Send a rider. I want him here.' Tenbridge hunkered beside the wheel of the chuck wagon as Crewle dispatched a man to the far side of the herd.

Chimm was riding swing. and he left the go-between to cover for him. It took him twenty minutes to get back to the trail camp, where Tenbridge was impatiently waiting for him. He swung his horse into the ropes of the remuda, tossing the reins towards a wrangler.

He was covered in trail dust, and looked surprised to see Tenbridge.

'What's goin' on Tusk? It's real early for you. Somethin' wrong?'

'Plenty,' Tenbridge growled. 'Lou Hollister rode into town last night.'

'Jeeesus,' Chimm muttered. 'What did he want?'

'He wanted to know who was ridin' one of his horses.' Briefly Tenbridge outlined what had happened in town. 'I think he'll be wantin' more than that now, though.'

Chimm looked dumbfounded. He took off his hat, and ran his fingers through his long, white hair.

'Timing,' he said. 'It's all about timing, Tusk. Hollister couldn't have got it better; just as we move the herd out.' He gave a half-smile to Crewle who was pounding out sourdough.

'You want that we hold up for a while?'

Tenbridge shook his head. 'We can't do that, Org. The buyers are wantin' their beef. We're on a promise. No delivery, no pay. But you'll have to leave a man or two behind to go after Hollister.'

'Our record's not that great with him, Tusk. You shouldn't o' let him see daylight, once you'd jailed him. As for Ricksen, you must o' know'd he was a one-time pal o' Hollister's.'

'Yeah, well that ain't gettin' us nowhere.' Tenbridge said. 'Those deputies were meant to take out both of 'em. They paid a lot for not doin' it.'

Under his breath, Chimm muttered something about Tenbridge paying a lot, then he spoke out to Stiles, Walter Henn and Brewster Zube.

'Hollister's got to be found, and he could be anywhere's from here to the Mexican Border.'

'Won't he try an' get to see his pa?' Stiles asked.

'Yeah, could be,' Chimm threw a glance at his colleague. 'You done anythin' about that?'

'Tusk thought o' that. I sent a man out to ol' Domus Kraal. Hollister'll get a fiery reception if he pokes his nose in there.'

'What happens if he don't? He knows he ain't got free rein around here.'

Tenbridge joined in. 'That's where you come in, Org. I want you to take a posse out for him. He's an escaped outlaw. He might not be alone. Think you can find him? Bring him in?'

Chimm looked amused. 'It'll be a cold day in Hell when I can't manage the likes of Hollister. Yeah, he won't be any trouble.'

'I doubt that,' Tenbridge suggested. He looked enquiringly at Chimm. 'What exactly was it between you and Hollister?'

'I thought you'd ask sooner or later,' Chimm said, his voice suddenly sounding curiously detached. 'I was a guard on one o' the Mississippi jail boats, then at the Vicksburg stockade. This Lou Hollister came aboard at Natchez with a small band o' Reb captives. Our rations were real poor, but theirs was worse, a lot worse. We traded 'em grub now and then for tobacco. Their shebangs always smelled o' the stuff. Anyways, I made a deal with Hollister to sell him some blankets. I made him pay up front, o' course. Only problem was, I wasn't goin' cold on his account.'

'Naturally. He remembered, did he?' Tenbridge taunted.

'He sure did. My boys had to drag him off me. He'd made some sort o' knife . . . would o' stuck me like a pig.'

'No professional courtesy there then.' Tenbridge snorted derisively.

'Yeah, well he paid for it, later. So did I. Latrine duty, then reassigned.'

Nobody said anything for a moment, but there were a few sidelong glances at Chimm.

Tenbridge pulled his hat off for a rub at his shining scalp.

'I want you to take young Loomis and the boys. Pick up his old man too. That should give you the most depraved and meanest bunch in Christendom. Just get Hollister. If you have to shoot him, shoot him.'

Chimm understood, and he looked confidently at the man giving orders.

The sun had disappeared now from the cold, bleak sky. Tenbridge gently patted the neck of Chimm's big grey.

'If he gets away this time Org, you'll be lookin' at more than a dose o' latrine duty. Now get movin'.'

11

PASADERA

Lou Hollister and Dooley Ricksen rode determined and hard. They made a long loop, keeping to the harder ground, careful not to raise dust. It was late afternoon when they crested a low bluff that overlooked the Pasadera ranch. Behind them, the peaks of the Sacramentos rose beckoningly against the western sky. But it wasn't to the west that Lou must turn his face. It was homeward he had to look, towards the house.

They dismounted to ease their horses, and take in the land ahead.

A wide reach of plain lay below them, where dogwood dotted the hard soil. Nestled in a brake of cottonwood was the livery stable, weathered sheds and low-walled adobe house of the Hollister family.

Lou just stared. It was the first time he'd seen his home in years. But he couldn't ride in. As of yesterday, he'd been outlawed. If the so-called 'law' was down there, they could shoot him from the saddle.

'Looks peaceable enough.' Dooley was holding his hand up against the low, wintry light. 'Don't reckon on it stayin' like that, if we ride in.'

Lou nodded at the suggestion, but he was looking south. 'Take a look there,' he said.

Dooley peered out to where a bunch of riders was breaking into file, walking their horses cautiously into the thick, mesquite.

'Who the hell are they?' he asked.

'Dunno, we'll have to get nearer,' Lou said.

Dooley climbed back into his saddle. 'Sometime, I'll have to get me a spyglass,' he muttered.

They walked down the bluff, then took narrow cuts through the rough dogwood. The scrub was thorny and high. It brushed their legs, and in places they couldn't see further than five or six paces ahead.

After close to an hour of pushing and winding through the thick dogwood, they broke cover. They were near to the house, and Lou gestured for caution.

From closer up it could be seen that neglect was beginning to touch the house. In parts, the adobe was breaking up, the porch steps were strewn with blowdown, the snake fencing around the small yard was collapsed. Two cowboys had appeared on the staging around the house, but there were no other signs of activity.

Dooley spoke very quietly. 'Where do you reckon the others are?'

'There's one way to find out, Dooley. They're there, I can smell 'em.'

'I'd rather I could see 'em. What you plannin', Lou?'

'I ain't come this far to ride on without seein' the old man.'

'You're not goin' to ride up to the front door?'

'Not without an advantage, I'm not.'

The two men sat quiet and alert on their horses. Lou was watching the scrub to the north. After ten minutes, he whistled short and sharp to get Dooley's attention. He pointed to his left.

'Out beyond the corral. It's them again.'

It was the group they'd seen earlier, riding into the thick mesquite. They'd now regrouped, headed for the broken fencing that partly screened the front of the ranch house. They appeared to be united and determined.

'I can see who they are now,' Dooley said. 'It's Alford Cropper with his boys.'

Lou recalled that the Croppers had originally been immigrant settlers from somewhere in the north of England. Since long before the war between the Northern and Southern states of America, they'd run cattle with the Hollisters and neighbouring ranchers. They'd always been a kindly and worthy family, and Lou wondered about the approaching confrontation on Pasadera land.

He watched them cross the open ground, loose-reined with rifles cradled in their arms. Alford led them in. He sat easy and proud, on a sturdy, golden-brown stallion.

Lou whispered gravidly: 'There's somethin' goin' on here we don't know about. I wonder if the

Croppers do?' He turned to Dooley, nodded back towards the brush. 'Let's move back aways.'

They backtracked, then circled until they neared the corral. Lou had a close look at the barn and bunkhouse. Both looked empty, but he didn't think they were. Like the other ranch buildings they were thick-walled, well fortified. He turned his attention back to the two men at the house.

He recognized one of them. A wild-looking man with a great fat beard. He had the set of middle-age, and wore filthy blue dungarees. He sat heavily in a deckchair and hawked a stream of tobacco juice between his boots.

'Domus Kraal,' Lou murmured, and tweaked his lips into a thin smile.

'Yeah, that's him,' Dooley agreed. 'When we was kids, we reckoned you could smell him up wind. The other one's a long rider from Del Rio. His name's Lem Brockway, and you wouldn't want to take him home with you.'

Lou was making a mental note of all he saw. After a full minute, his mind made up, he turned to Dooley.

'That's a Henry repeater you've got there, Dooley. Mind if I borrow it a while?'

Dooley pulled the rifle from it's scabbard and swung the stock towards Lou. He looked concerned as Lou levered a shell into the chamber.

'You aim to take 'em both from here?'

Lou smiled back at him.

'No. I'm for heading off the Croppers. They could be the advantage we need.'

Lou turned his horse back towards the brush, but he was too late.

Kraal and Brockway had moved back inside the house. A moment later, Alford Cropper's horse stepped assuredly from behind the snake fencing into the front yard of the house.

After a slow advance of twenty yards Alford Cropper checked the buckskin. He turned to his eldest son.

'We're close enough, Barton. Take your brothers back into the brush. I'm doin' this alone. Give me cover if it's needed.'

Barton's face burned with indignation.

'You're not doin' this alone. They'll kill you if we're not together.'

Alford stopped his son with a penetrating look.

'My mind's made up. Do as I say, Barton.' Barton felt the grip of frustration, but he glared at his brothers and obediently dug his heels into his horse.

The buckskin threw its head into the air and snickered with insecurity. Alford held his rifle in one hand, kept a light, close rein with the other. His eyes tunneled straight ahead, looking for any sign of ambush.

He drew the horse in, swung the rifle back to the crook of his arm and faced the ranch house door.

'Clewson. Clew Hollister,' he called.

There was no response, and Alford glanced around him. He sensed danger, as a dog senses fear. From inside the house, a bolt was thrown, and he pointed the rifle towards the door.

A figure moved into the doorway. Clewson

68

Hollister sat hunched in his invalid chair, clutching a stick. His eyes were staring level and hostile at Alford.

'What do you want with me? Get off my land.'

With equally bitter feeling, Alford addressed the aged rancher.

'Tell me about the men who killed my son, then I'll get off your land.'

Clewson Hollister was instantly, visibly shocked.

'I know nothin' of a killing. Your son, you say?'

'Harlsey, my youngest one.' Alford tried hard to keep the authority. 'We found him yesterday. He was lying face down in the gully with a bullet in his chest. The water is still running red across your land, Clew. The men that murdered him ride from here.'

Clewson dropped his stick, and his pale fingers clawed at the arms of his chair. His grizzled jaw trembled.

'Whatever's happening here, it don't involve killin' children. You have my word on that, Alford. Little Harlsey, you say. I'm so sorry, I don't—'

Alford saw the breakdown of Clewson Hollister's hostility, and he cut short the old man's anguish.

'An' I'm sorry for what happened to you, Clew. But that's small peas now. You're responsible.'

Clewson's voice was hardly audible. 'You're sure they were from here?'

'I'm sure,' Alford said, levelly. 'They were pushin' cattle, a lot of 'em mine. Harlsey ran into 'em, and they shot him down. My son, Preston, found his body. Together we trailed 'em to one of your corrals. It wasn't hard. We saw 'em workin' on the branding . . . from *my* Teeside to *your* Pasadera.'

Alford turned his head slightly. 'You know nothin' of that, I'm guessin'?'

Before there was any further response, sounds of a noisy dispute broke from inside the house. Clewson Hollister turned his chair away from the doorway, and Alford pulled back the buckskin sharply.

Both men heard someone cursing loudly before another voice cut the air.

'I can shoot you where you stand, Kraal.'

12

SHANKS'S MARE

There was a pause, a deep, rumbling cough, a sneer. Then a booming gunshot punched across the room behind the front door.

Within the instant crush of dead sound that followed, the girl's voice again rang clear.

'You cowardly scum. I'll kill you. He's riding away from here, now. Get out there and tell them.'

Domus Kraal and Lem Brockway moved back on to the stoop. The girl followed closely, her face ashen, her eyes dark and flaming. She was pointing a .38 Quickloader, which Lou immediately recognized.

He was in the mesquite, watching. He gritted his teeth as the girl shoved the gleaming barrel at Kraal.

'Do it,' she yelled at him. 'Tell them, he's to ride away. I'll send you to hell now, if you don't.'

Kraal raised his voice in alarm. 'Get Cropper out o' here, boys. She means it.'

Cowboys shambled from the bunkhouse into the yard. Some were sniggering, but they were all fascinated by the sight of Domus Kraal stuck on the end of Tess's carbine. Rough, jingo Texans had their own ideas about a woman's place.

One of them called out, but because of the situation, it lacked conviction.

'An' if we don't, you cain't be shootin' us all, ma'am.'

Tess tossed her hair and sniffed. 'I don't aim to, *mister*. This growth gets it first, then it'll be your turn. Now go ahead. Make up your mind.'

The Kraal method of staying alive was to know when to back off.

'It's the jailbreaker we want, boys.' Kraal spat out the words drily. 'An' I got a feelin' she'll use this popgun that's stuck between my shoulder blades. You let Cropper ride in safe enough. Now we can all watch him ride out the same way,' he added with bite.

Just behind Kraal, Lem Brockway said:

'We can take care o' him some other time.' The man from Del Rio smirked and took a step towards Tess.

Kraal glowered at Alford Cropper.

'You heard, English. Clear out.'

Alford removed his hat, and ran his fingers through silver-stubbled hair. His eyes blistered Kraal, then settled on the girl.

'Thank you, girl. Come and visit an old man sometime.' He nodded courteously.

As he cantered out of the yard, Kraal called after him:

'We'll all come and visit.'

All eyes followed Alford, and Tess relaxed a little.

She allowed the barrel of the carbine to drop, and Brockway siezed the opportunity. He lashed out, gripped the gun, and wrenched it from Tess's hands.

'Now then, you pretty little bitch,' he breathed into her face, 'let's hear what you've got to say about this.'

But the threat was hardly uttered, before Kraal jumped him.

'Gimme the gun,' he shouted, slamming his elbow into Brockway's ribs. Then with an ugly oath, he swept the barrel into line with Alford Cropper's retreating back.

For all his furious haste, Kraal wasn't fast enough to make the shot. The noise of a Henry repeating rifle crashed out across the yard, and behind Kraal a window expoded into a thousand fragments. There was no time for anyone on the stoop to move, before Lou's voice followed up.

'Drop the gun, Kraal. Throw it into the yard.'

As shattered as the window, Kraal gasped. He didn't understand quickly enough, and stared straight ahead. Then his eyes jumped around, looking for the gunman in the brush. He tossed the carbine out in front of him, and Lou called again:

'Don't get foolhardy. I can kill any one o' you from here.'

'Who the hell's that?' Kraal glared swiftly at Brockway, who'd been considering a move.

Kraal was breathing heavily, shaking with confusion, but he retained the survival instinct.

'I'm Lou Hollister,' Lou shouted. 'Tenbridge's jailbreaker. The man you've been waitin' for.' A spiky silence followed before Lou spoke again. 'You two men, take a good look at the window behind you – then unbuckle your gunbelts.'

Lou shifted the rifle sights between Kraal and Brockway. If one of them was going to break the stand-off, he wasn't sure who it would be. They were pushed and unpredictable. He remained tense, his finger gently feeling the trigger.

Kraal said something to Brockway, and they removed their guns. Kraal swung his belt out alongside him, and Brockway let his drop around his feet.

Lou whistled low through his teeth. He'd have preferred a better time for getting involved, but Kraal's attempt at backshooting Alford Cropper gave him no choice.

He started at a snap and crackle behind him, turned his head fractionally as a horse nosed forward. Dooley Ricksen appeared, shifting through the tangled mesquite.

'I got to the Croppers,' Dooley said uneasily. 'They're all ready, if you need 'em.'

'Let's find out,' Lou said. Without taking his eyes off Kraal and Brockway, he yelled towards the ranch house. 'You're all trespassin' on Hollister land. Get off it now, before I decide to kill somebody.'

As Lou rose and stepped forward the yard was suddenly bordered with horsemen. It was Alford Cropper and his boys, bristling with weapons. Dooley crabbed his horse close alongside Lou.

Domus Kraal took a step forward, wiping a stained hand across his mouth.

'Lou Hollister. I should o' guessed,' he said resignedly. 'Come back for a wash and brush up, eh?'

'Yeah, well it's somethin' you'd never know about, Kraal,' Lou answered roughly. 'You'll always smell like the tail end of a buffalo. An' talkin' o' that, when you see your boy, Loomis, you can tell him I'm comin' for him. Him and Chimm.'

Kraal dragged out a scornful threat.

'Loomis's no angel, Hollister, but he's my son, and he's no killer. You'll have to go through me.'

Lou stared coldly across the yard, as he walked slowly forward.

'Your boy knows how a kid out huntin' rabbits gets slaughtered, and somebody's goin' pay for the death o' my brother. Goin' through you's just an option.'

'We ain't talkin' piss an' wind, Hollister. You've fallen into the rattler pit.'

Lou stepped up tight to Kraal.

'Well then, snake breath, I'll make the most of what time's left.'

Without taking his eyes from the man's face, Lou swung the barrel of his rifle across Kraal's shins. Kraal yelled in pain and as he went down to grab his legs Lou slammed his bunched knuckles hard into the side of his head.

'I'm tired o' your mouth, Kraal. Now stay down-wind, and get off this land.'

As Kraal and Brockway slouched towards the corral, Dooley Ricksen looked up from collecting the gunbelts.

'Hey,' he called out. 'How you gettin' back to town?'

Both men stared back at him.

'Can't see any of your horses in the corral.' Dooley looked at Lou and smiled. 'There's only Pasadera mounts in there.'

The implication dawned on Brockway.

'It's twenty five miles to Toya Bend.'

'I'd say closer to thirty. Without guns an' horses, you'll be mighty hard-pressed. I doubt if you'll make it for breakfast,' Dooley snapped.

As the men began their walk out into the brush Alford Cropped watched from his buckskin. He was curt, but as civil as he'd been to Tess.

'It's not somethin' I'm used to, friend, but I'm in your debt,' he said. 'We'll meet soon, to talk about the future. Now, my sons and I have to drive that herd of animals off your land.' Then a callous edge crept into his voice. 'I still need to know how Harlsey died. Perhaps between here and the town, someone will tell me. Who knows?' Cropper touched the brim of his hat respectfully.

Lou watched them go. He turned to Dooley.

'Somethin' tells me Cropper's goin' to find out who shot his boy. So there ain't goin' to be much of a future for *them*,' he said.

13

THE HOLLISTER FAMILY

When Lou walked on to the stoop, his shoulders hunched, Teresa was waiting. By the look in her eyes it was obvious the shock had got to her.

'Ma'am,' he said, uncertain of the full name, or the use of Tess. 'I see you found my old Quickloader.'

Her mouth was trembling as she tried for a response.

'I know how to use a gun. Kraal was going to shoot Mr Cropper through the window.'

'Through his *head*, more likely.' Lou smiled at his little joke. 'An' if you'd really known how to shoot, you'd have taken it off.'

Tess smiled, and it broke the approach. 'So you're Lou?'

'Yeah, that's him,' a voice rattled from just inside the door. 'He don't visit much.'

Lou looked in at his father. He expected to see a

physical change, but the old man in the Bath chair was a long way off the Clewson Hollister he remembered. In the haggard terrain of his father's face, only the long nose remained as a landmark.

'Dad?' he said, staring at the tortuous clasp of his father's hands.

The aged rancher sat scowling.

'Where the hell you been? It's been years.'

Lou's emotions were confused, and he went for a vague response.

'Most places . . . border points . . . looked over the edges.'

Clewson rubbed at his grizzled chin. 'Well you don't look like you got rich in the lookin'. What you doin' with them Croppers? You come back to take me off as well?'

'What have the Cropper's taken from you, Dad? From what I hear, it sounds like it's Pasadera that's been on the grab.'

'No. They're all stealin' from me.' The old man was shaking with his indiscriminate anger. 'Them Croppers have been helpin' themselves. They're no better than . . . than . . .' Clewson's attitude changed slightly. 'I know nothin' about the boy, Harlsey. I swear it.'

'I believe that, Dad. But Tenbridge knew about it. He knew about Tench too.' Lou gave his father a penetrating look. 'What's all this really about? It's more than cattle rustlin'. They've got something else. They're runnin' the ranch as if it's theirs.'

Clewson banged his hands on his knees, but looked defiant.

'You come back here, after all these years, and without so much as a word. You start tellin' me what's so. There's ways of skinnin' a cat. Learn some,' he snapped.

Lou saw the torture within his old man, and knew he'd hit a raw nerve. He also felt a gnawing fear of the unknown.

'You can tell me about it,' he said tentatively. 'Your story, not what I'm surmisin'.'

The shadow of a near-forgotten smile crossed Clewson's face. He turned around, and looked over to where Teresa was standing, tactful and quiet.

'Yeah, this is the youngest one, Tess. Lou.' He looked back up at Lou. 'Tess's been the daughter I never had. Don't know what I'd do without her, now.'

Lou eased his way into the room.

'Perhaps you won't have to,' he muttered.

Tess glanced at the men's faces, and blinked a few times.

'I know,' she said. 'We're all starved.'

Clewson turned on Dooley Ricksen, and his eyes narrowed.

'You ain't been invited.'

Lou's chin sunk to his chest, and he swore, exasperated. He glared at his father.

'It was Dooley got me out o' jail. Christ, there's some rotten peel around you.'

Dooley was already backing away, towards the stoop.

Lou stepped towards him. 'I know how you feel,' he said. 'Perhaps I should never have come back. Let's go.'

As they made towards the yard Clewson ran his chair against the door post.

'Goddamn it, you only just arrived,' he yelled.

Dooley turned. 'I've never done anythin' to harm you or yours, Mr Hollister, and you know it.' He looked sadly at Lou, and carried on towards his horse.

Lou turned back to Clewson. 'Yeah, Tench and Dooley took some beef. Beef that had already been stole from the ranchers round here. They sold it back to 'em, for a dollar a head.'

'They sold 'em back?' Clewson queried.

'That's right, Mr Hollister, you included,' Dooley joined in. 'Ranch owners got some cattle back, and me an' Tench made a few dollars. We was kids, an' we earned it.'

'Tusk Tenbridge knew about this, did he? He found out?'

'Yeah,' Dooley said. 'He found out. That's the real reason behind Tench getting shot. If I'd been with him, they'd have got me too.'

Clewson looked at both men and for many moments no one said a word. Then he wrinkled his nose and pushed himself back inside the house.

'That's as maybe,' they heard him say. 'Can't help it if I heard different.'

Lou shrugged his shoulders, raised his eyebrows at Dooley.

'Well, now we got the apologies over with, let's see if that food's anywhere near ready. I'm getting real tired o' stock-feed.'

14

THE IDLE TALK

Once he was inside the main room of the house the nostalgia immediately crowded in on Lou.

There was the French piano, a Victorian writing-desk, a dresser filled with blue-patterned china, a big, scrubbed-pine table and a dozen and one other small reminders of a better past. All of it freighted to this remote, Texas wilderness by his father. Most of it had been to please Lou's mother, in a land so harsh and different from her Southern upbringing.

He looked at the big mantel over the stone fire-place. He'd never forgotten the stern pictures that had watched him all these years. One, huge and oval-framed of his grandfather, the other, smaller and even more severe, of his father. But it all brought back the carefree, spirited memories of his childhood.

During the meal conversation was still strained, but a little easier than it had been. After they'd eaten Lou sat on the stoop with his father. Dooley tactfully stayed inside.

'Tell me about you breakin' out o' jail,'

'How I got in there's more interestin',' Lou

answered. 'They'd have killed me. It wasn't the first time. Dooley turned the tables on 'em.'

'How'd you get tangled with Tenbridge in the first place?'

'I didn't. It wasn't him in the first place.' Lou told his story, while his father sat, engrossed, but uncomfortable. He told of the confrontation in Cuidad Blanco and the attempt on his life after being trailed. 'That's where Tenbridge turned up, spoke of me being a Hollister, or not.' Lou looked keenly at his father. 'You know what he meant by that, don't you, Dad?'

'I know what he meant,' Clewson growled. 'You've probably guessed most of it. He's set to take over the ranch, an' there's not much I can do about it. I'm financially ruined.' Clewson looked hollow-eyed at Lou. 'But there's somethin' else.'

Lou detected helpless suffering as his father carried on. 'There's somethin' he's stringin' me out with.' He paused, adjusting to his misery. 'It's about your mother and Tess. Tenbridge claims to have somethin' on her.'

'Somethin' on her?' Lou repeated incredulously. 'Sounds like a tick on a saddle? Who's he got somethin' on?'

'Tess. But it goes back to your mother. He reckons Tess's *her* daughter. It would have happened in Jonesboro. That's near Atlanta, Georgia.'

'Yeah, I know where Atlanta is. An' you believe all this? You had no idea?'

'No. How could I? No reason to suspect. I never knew her then, o' course. I couldn't have known.'

'What proof's Tenbridge got? Has he told you that?'

'That's what he knows . . . what he says.'

'Tess's my sister?'

'Half-sister. Yes.'

'Does she know?'

'She don't know a thing. Anyone who knows the truth will be dead an' buried by now. That's why he gets his own way. Can you get a handle on that?'

'Yeah, I think so. Has he threatened to tell her?'

'No.'

'Did it hurt bad, when you found out?'

'Not by the time I began to believe it. There was always a streak there, the way she looks, sometimes.'

Lou looked back into the house, but didn't think they were being overheard.

'I can see what you meant by the "daughter you never had".' He suddenly looked at his father suspiciously. 'You don't think there's anythin' between 'em, do you?'

'Who? Tess and Tenbridge? Hell, no. But it may be something he's got his mind on.'

'You must have thought o' shootin' him, Dad?'

'Every time I see him.'

Clewson and Lou sat quiet, both with their own thoughts. Lou knew how ordinary folk responded to hearsay. They weren't as big on tolerance as they were on bigotry in that part of the West. Tess would carry a stigma, and it would reflect back on Clewson. It would be simple enough in the telling, but the result would be cruel and lasting.

Clewson went on to tell what he knew of the past. But Lou wasn't listening. He was trying to get his mind set on what to do.

Clewson poked a bony finger into Lou's leg. His voice had recovered a touch of its former grittiness.

'Like I said, she's been here while you were gone. There was no one else.'

'Yeah, I understand,' Lou spoke quietly. 'There's no argument with that.'

There was another silence, then Clewson said:

'What's to do, son? Seems like we're in a hell of a mess. Your prospects ain't much if you stay here.'

Lou touched his father's shoulder. 'Whatever it takes, Dad. You ain't the only one with trouble on his back. I'll be leavin' shortly. I'll take Dooley.'

'Where you goin'?'

'Tenbridge's packing a herd up to Cuidad Blanco. That's where we'll make a start.' Briefly, Lou explained what was on his mind, and Clewson listened, growing tired and bemused.

'With help, you might get away with it.' Clewson nodded thoughtfully to himself. 'I'll get you a note on ownership. You'll need it.'

Clewson turned and wheeled himself back into the house. It had been dark a long time, and Lou sat with his back against the cool adobe wall and fretted. He sensed a movement close behind him and turned his head. Tess was looking up at the moon, which gleamed, wafer-thin.

He couldn't think of anything to say. He thought of some of the mush that Dooley had been delivering earlier, then realized he was staring at her.

'Hi. Come to have a look at the night,' he said. The situation made it difficult for him, and Tess didn't know why.

She said, 'I was going to say, you look worried, but decided not to. It would have been pretty dumb. For what it's worth, Lou, I'm glad you came back. I don't suppose you can tell, but your pa already looks better. Some of his spirit's returned.'

'I never knew about the accident.'

'That's when he got worse. When he became suspicious of his friends. Sometimes, I think he includes me in his darkness.' Tess's voice began to break with emotion. 'You will help, won't you? He won't come out and say it, but he needs you. We both do. There's no one else to turn to.'

Clewson rolled out on to the stoop between them. With a curious look of concern he broke into their talk.

'Smelled burnin' from somewhere near, turned out to be my own ears.' He sounded sarcastic, but his tone wasn't aggressive or provocative.

Tess went back into the house, and Clewson held up a piece of paper for Lou.

'Here's your note. It gives you authority on the herd and the ranch. Keep it safe. I'm off to bed now. Goodnight, son.' That was all he had to say. He shivered from the night cold that blew across the range, and went back inside.

Alone in the darkness, Lou shoved the written document into his coat and forgot it. He was still thinking of Tess and his mother, but there was another problem.

When it was known where he'd been, and what he'd done in the years since Vicksburg, he'd rank alongside Tess. His father was wrong about being in a hell of a mess. It was far worse.

85

15

PARTNER

Lou Hollister and Dooley Ricksen left the house well
before sun-up. The land still held its severe night
chill, its breezes cutting through the frosty mesquite.
They rode, side by side. Sometimes the horses closed
up, other times the dense brush wedged their trails
apart. The men, each with his own thoughts, were
wrapped in silence until the dawn yielded the clam-
our of aroused wildlife.

Lou had his doubts about leaving Pasadera unde-
fended. It worried him, but he didn't believe
Tenbridge would actually order retribution, or that
Clewson or Tess were in immediate danger.
Tenbridge knew what he wanted, but it didn't mean
he'd run himself ragged for the sake of a few days. It
was different for him and Dooley, though. By now,
they could be printed-up members of a gang of
outlaws; prey to anyone who carried a gun.

Dooley was taking Lou to see a friend, a modest
cattle rancher and a breaker of mustangs for the

86

army. As grey light fused into blue, they skirted tangles of dogwood, saw the small ranch and it's outbuildings higgledy-piggledy in the bend of a creek.

Dooley Ricksen greeted the man, who'd seen their trail dust from a long way off. He was introduced as Ben Finch, a slim, muscular man, dressed in worn denim and leather chaps.

Lou and Dooley sat drinking coffee on the low step outside Ben's logged cabin. Ben sat on a stump, telling of how, and more than once, he'd surprised someone driving off a few of his precious longhorns or a saddle-broke mustang. Not much in Texas terms, but to Ben the difference between sink or swim.

'They were Tenbridge's men?' asked Lou.

'Can't be certain, but who else could they be?' Ben said. 'Only Tenbridge could put together a big, made-up herd. He could provide the protection you'd need.'

'Got any plans?' Lou asked.

'Yeah. I'm goin' to wait till day don't follow night, then I'm goin' to creep in an' get my stock back.' Ben shrugged his shoulders. 'What plannin' can you do, when you're so much out on your own?'

Lou nodded understandingly and thought for a moment.

'Don't stay out on your own. Join me an' Dooley. What have you got to lose?'

'You've somethin' in mind?'

'Yeah. I'm gonna hit Tenbridge. When the time's right I could use some help. With you, we'll be up to three.'

Ben made a wry smile. 'You just asked, what I'd got to lose? With those odds, it'd probably be my life.'

Dooley spoke up. 'We'll get more. There must be more ranchers who lost stock to Tenbridge's men. There's the Croppers to begin with. They've lost many a head. I reckon the old man gritted his teeth for the sake of a quiet life. But they made a mistake in killing little Harlsey. Alford an' his boys won't ever let that rest.'

'Yeah. You've got yourself another gun if you want it.' Ben declared his hand. 'How you fixin' to hit him?' he went on. 'I can get some help. Rex Newton'll join us. He's just lost a string o' yearlin's.'

Lou stood up. 'Tenbridge's organizin' a drive up to Cuidad Blanco. From what I've seen an' heard, Tenbridge calls the tune in most of Cottonwood County. He rubs with the army and the damn carpet-baggers. But he's still got to drive that herd to Cuidad Blanco. There's no law to speak of west of the plateau. Even the Texas Rangers give it room.'

Dooley jumped to his feet alongside Lou.

'That's it. We hit him out on the plateau. We'll pay him back some.'

'It won't be a junket, Dooley. Those men of his are hard an' mean, an' they ain't too bothered about who's in the right.'

The men looked at each other enthusiastically.

Lou said to Ben, 'After we've called up your man, Newton, we'll ride to the Cropper ranch.'

'Good,' Ben replied. Then he nodded to his cabin. 'Come on, I'll cook us up some breakfast before we go. I've a clutch of fresh hen's eggs.'

*

The men dismounted on a slanting bluff. They stood, holding in their horses, looking north. From miles away, a shadow of dust billowed low where the herd spilled like dark crumbs atop a bleached table.

'Early tomorrow will be a good time,' suggested Alford Cropper, his gaze fixed on the cloud ahead. 'Tomorrow, or maybe—'

'No maybes,' Lou Hollister said quickly. 'We're runnin' out o' time. We'll hit 'em while they're still off the border.'

He watched the slow-moving herd. For days they'd followed, skirted the Edwards Plateau, keeping well out of sight. Lou knew they had to make their move before the herd crossed into Oklahoma. An attack there could easily run them up against soldiers out of a Red River fort.

That far, they'd let Tusk Tenbridge's trail crew drift the cattle north, but it would only be *that* far. Once again, he considered their chances. The Tenbridge outfit was made up of ten riders. Lou was going up against them with Dooley Ricksen, Ben Finch, Rex Newton, Alford Cropper and his three boys. They were down in numbers, but courage and surprise might even it up a bit, he thought. If it didn't, it was the wind up for him, and everyone else.

'We'll make our last camp below the next ridge,' he said. 'Cold harbour, not even coffee. I want everyone ready early. We'll take them just before sun-up.'

'Where will you be, then?' asked Dooley.

'The cattle will be bedded down soon. I'm goin' to

take a wide swing east, then north. Have a closer look at the land. I'll be back sometime after dark.'

Lou rode east. He kept hidden, making gain from every rib of land around the plateau. He used his eyes well, seeking firmer ground, close in to wind-blown rises and tangles of brush. It was a rider's way, and Lou understood it.

He found where the herd would be settled for the night. The chuckwagon was ahead, unhitched, and pointing north, bankside to the Santa Rosa Lake. Lou sat and quartered the land. The gully was edged with shrubby birch and willow. Bunchgrass was scattered in thin clumps around the rested chuckwagon.

Lou loose-hobbled his horse, and crawled through the grass to within fifty feet of the wagon. The cook was limping around the new fire, laying a skillet and pulling cans from the store-box. He was making ready for camp supper, and Lou watched him shaping curses that went with the task. They'd all have something to complain about early next morning, he was thinking.

He looked out at the herd coming in. The point riders were already turning the lead steers into their milling rest. He'd seen enough then, and he crawled along the gully bank a-ways, even managed to pull up a root for the gelding.

Time was moving on, shadows were merging into the flat greyness of evening. To the east, where Dooley Ricksen should be setting out a cold harbour camp, the scrub-covered ridge was just touching the sun as it settled into the range.

16

BARE KNUCKLE

Lou had ridden back three or four miles when he heard the unmistakable sound of gunfire crack the range. He pulled in his horse to listen, and heard two more gunshots before silence closed in again. His heartbeat quickened as he realized the firing came from the direction of their camp, near the still-distant ridge. With a sinking gut feeling he shouted, and raced his horse.

Running at speed, using the throw of the land for cover, was something Lou knew about. He'd learned the hard way, where grisly torture or death often awaited a mistake. Riding frontier mail routes was good for the learning, if you live long enough to profit by it.

For nearly a mile he tore along the bed of the gully, before swinging his horse out onto the low bank. There was a clearing ahead of him with no brush cover; but without slowing, he drove hard across it. The horse's hoofs pounded the soil; the only sounds Lou noticed, until they joined the thudding discord of fast-closing riders.

He had the time to swing around, but only back into the shallow cover of the gully. He had to go forward, to try and make the slope with its scrub cover. Camp should be somewhere in the lee of the ridge, less than a quarter-mile. A few more minutes was all he needed.

He never made the cover. In the closing darkness the riders came at him. There were two of them, but Lou couldn't make out any feature. They were on to him, too sudden, and from astride a pale horse one of them had already levelled his gun. It exploded within twenty paces of Lou as he pulled his Colt.

With the report of the gunshot crashing around his head, Lou didn't slow. He rode on, until at point-blank range he shot into the body of the man who'd fired. There was a tormented whinny, then he cannoned on, into the second rider. The mare shuddered and reeled from the impact of muscle, but Lou regained control as the other horse and rider fell to the ground. He swerved away, but from close distance turned and sat for a moment while his own horse took in great lungfuls of air. He watched as the man who'd been thrown scrambled clear of his saddle and stirrups. Lou actioned his Colt again, as the shaken rider looked for the rifle he'd been carrying.

The fallen horse lurched back to its feet, its eyes bulging with fright and its body trembling. The rider looked around nervously, then walked slowly to where his partner was lying dead.

Lou edged his horse up behind the man.

'Don't make any more dumb moves, mister, unless you want to join him,' Lou snapped. 'Tell me who you are, an' what you're doin' here.'

The man got to his feet slowly and gaped up at Lou. He glanced at the ground around him.

'I'm not certain,' he answered doubtfully. He was trying to get himself together, trying to figure out a credible line. 'We were out lookin' to make camp. You know the rest.'

Lou almost laughed.

'Yeah, and I was takin' the air.' He nodded at the man on the ground.

'He dead?'

'From that close, he was dead before he hit the ground,' was the sour response.

'A hell of way to make camp,' Lou muttered. 'Now, I've already asked you once, What're you doin' out here?'

The man took a long, deep-rasping breath. 'Scoutin' for Pasadera. We're on the drive to Cuidad Blanco.'

Lou got a short stab of pain behind his temple, and swallowed hard. 'What was the gunfire, back along the ridge?'

'We been keepin' watch on riders that been doggin' the herd. Been south of us for days. We caught up with 'em. Shot their camp up a bit.'

Lou's heart was thumping with anguish. 'Make a fight back, did they, or did you get 'em cold?'

The man was unnerved by the manner of Lou's interest.

93

'Peck figured he hit one or two, but weren't sure. There was more of 'em than we thought. I'm paid for scoutin', not gunfightin'.'

Lou wanted to know more, wondered who Peck was.

'What made you think they were after the herd?'

'Pasadera sent out a rider to warn us. Mr Tenbridge said to look out for riders that came too close. Man called Hollister would probably be at the head of 'em.'

The man stopped suddenly, and looked curiously at Lou. 'Who the hell are *you*, mister?'

'Hollister. Lou Hollister, an' that'll be my father that owns Pasadera, not Mr Tenbridge, as you seem to think.' Lou dismounted and walked straight to the man. 'Now there's one or two things to clear up, scoutin' man.' He kicked out at the scout's kneecaps, and watched coldly as the man sank painfully to his knees.

Lou took a step back. 'I've told you who *I* am; now who the hell are *you*, scout, and who's in charge out there?'

The man was back on his feet. He held out his hands submissively, in a slow and awkward movement. 'They call me Moss. I'm a scout for the drive. That's all I was hired for,' he said, but it was only a deception for what the man had in mind.

The open palm of his right hand suddenly clenched tight, and he swung his fist upwards, aiming for Lou's face.

But Lou had sensed the movement, and before it plugged in he sidestepped. Moss stumbled forward.

He was temporarily off balance, and Lou ripped a quick blow up and into his head. It was vicious, and cracked Moss's nose, immediately spurting flecks of dark blood across his face.

Moss snorted and his legs buckled as he dragged air into his throat. His eyes were eager and glaring, and Lou quickly hit him again. It was like punching wood, and pain shot along his arm and right shoulder. Moss was enraged and stamped forward, ignoring the blows. He was rough and strong, even sneering as he came on. He flung his arms wide to draw Lou into him. Lou flat-footed two, then three steps backwards. He waited until Moss rushed, then with both fists swung hard. He almost lost his footing, and it wasn't enough to put Moss down.

Moss squeezed his eyes, then bluffed left to swing a hard loop with his right arm. Lou was surprised, and took a lot of the pain on his forearm, but the fist smashed sharp and severe into his ribs. He blinked several times as the shock wave pulsed across his chest. It was momentary, but in the distraction another blow smacked into his forehead. It sent him toppling down hard and flat on his shoulder blades. He drew his knees in close, and rolled sideways as Moss came leaping in. He was cursing and stomping with a boot heel, hoping to thrust the rasping wedge somewhere into Lou's face. The kick grated across Lou's scalp, and as he pushed himself to his feet, Moss moved towards him.

The scout came in again, and Lou stood his ground, watching the reckless bending swing of the man's fist. It was easy to dodge, and Lou stepped inside, making a hard stab into the knotted flesh of Moss's neck.

Moss gasped for breath, and threw out his arms wildly. He locked his fingers around Lou's back, clutching them tight against his spine. The pressure got worse, and Moss crushed the pungent sweat of his body into Lou's face.

Lou felt himself being lifted off his feet, and he struggled to keep his heels on the ground. His arms and legs were losing their control, and as his breath became shallow, he twisted his head away from the vile closeness of the scout.

As Lou wearied himself into submission, Moss mistook the effect of his grip and relaxed his hold slightly; long enough for Lou to respond and wrench his arms free. Without pausing he threw his hands under Moss's jaw and jerked upwards. Moss immediately tried to tighten his arms, but Lou had the advantage. He straightened his hand and snapped his knuckles into the point of Moss's Adam's apple. The man instantly fell away, writhing with soundless agony as he clutched at his throat.

Moss began making odd retching noises as he shambled around Lou. He spread his arms and they weaved slowly, cobralike, trying to catch Lou's eye. He got closer and closer, then kicked out, his foot catching Lou in the right knee. The blow sent Lou sprawling, and he spread-eagled, landing with his face shoved into the hard, trampled ground.

Lou twisted on to his back and kicked out with his feet at the blurred figure of Moss. But the blow connected, his heels driving hard into the bone of kneecaps. The impact felled Moss like a woodsman's axe, and he fell with an arm stretched across Lou's waist. Before he could recover, Lou bounded to his feet and smashed his bunched fist down at the arch of Moss's neck. Then he drove short chopping blows into the man's sinewy shoulders.

Moss tried to draw his knees up, but failed and collapsed as another blow took him full and low in the back. He rolled from side to side, trying to extricate himself, spitting blood from his smashed mouth as Lou stood over him. He managed to unwind into a crouch, his face and hair smeared with sweat and masked with dirt. He swayed and trod himself into a tight circle while Lou took a step backwards.

'Now, I'll ask you again. Who's runnin' that herd?' Lou rasped.

Moss spat into the ground. 'Walter Games. They're all Tenbridge's men. Me an' Peck were the only ones that weren't. I already told you.'

'One other thing.' Lou winced at his bruised ribs. 'This word you had from Toya Bend? Was there mention of back-up for Games?'

The scout looked as though he'd had enough talk, but as Lou took a painful, impatient breath, he spluttered back a response.

'They're sendin' a posse out. Organ Chimm's ridin' with it.'

'Chimm,' Lou repeated, thoughtfully.

'Yeah. You've met him, have you?' The spite was plain in Moss's voice.

'We've met,' said Lou. The anger burst from him as he turned away from the scout. 'Get back to the herd,' he yelled. 'When you get there, tell Games to expect a visit real soon. Tell him, Lou Hollister's coming to take his herd back.'

Lou rode away to the ridge. He kicked his heels deep, his insides knotted with the dread of what he'd find.

17

DEATH CAMP

There was nobody in sight when Lou rode close to the camp. It was fully dark as he twisted silently through the clumps of brush. He stared into the darkness, but couldn't see much, save the black silhouettes of cottonwood.

He eased his Colt from his waistband, gave a short, sharp whistle, and waited for a response. After a minute or two, a sound, then a movement caught his attention, and he made a cautious, muffled call.

'Over here.'

A rider stepped his horse forward, and spoke quietly.

'That you, Lou? We been expectin' you.'

It was Dooley Ricksen. Lou eased forward to meet him.

'What happened, Dooley?'

'They rode in on us, less than an hour ago. Just started shootin'. Stockton Cropper took most of it. Ben got hit.'

'How bad?'

'Ben'll live, but Stockton's real bad.'

Lou didn't say anything except, 'Show me, where.'

Dooley swung his horse around, and Lou followed. He was wondering what to say, thinking of his blunder in leaving the men alone. He hadn't considered that Walter Games would have a scout, and that they'd been watched ever since leaving Cottonwood County. While he'd gone to poke his nose around the range, they'd taken the time to shoot up his own men. He swore savagely, and looked to the stars.

Dooley stopped and turned his head. 'What's up?' he called back.

Lou rode alongside. 'Sorry, I was just thinkin' aloud. Tell me how it happened.'

'Stockton was supposed to be on watch. Wasn't his fault though. Wouldn't have been much trouble to gun him down. They knew what they were doin'. *He* didn't, poor kid.'

Lou made a sharp, guttural sound in his throat, and Dooley carried on explaining.

'He managed to shoot back, though. None of us knew what was goin' on. We were firin' into the night. Couldn't see nothin' 'cept the powder flashes.'

'What happened then?'

'They must o' rode off.' Dooley could see Lou's face, pale in the darkness. 'We heard a couple o' gunshots sometime after. Was that you, Lou?'

Lou was already thinking on how he'd let the second man off with his life, how he'd sent him back with the message to Games. But he hadn't known for sure then what had happened. He told Dooley the story of the run-in and his fight.

Dooley looked hard again at Lou's face.

'Yeah I thought there was somethin' wrong. You all right?'

Lou avoided the question.

'Chimm's after us with a posse.'

'You want we should call it off?'

It was about the only thing that made sense to Lou. They'd lost another rider, and Games would soon be joined by Chimm and his men. Lou's strategy was beginning to look like the broken straight.

'I can't ask any of you to do any more, Dooley. I'll finish it alone if I have to.'

'No need. Alford's in no frame o' mind to ride away. We've already decided, Lou. We'll all of us stay for as long as it takes.'

Night wind scuffled the brush as they rode in the lee of the ridge. The creak of tack and snorting from the horses were the only sounds that broke the silence. After a few hundred yards Dooley pulled up and called into the darkness. A voice replied, and they dismounted.

A small fire burned in the blowdown and colourless scrub. In the margins of firelight, figures were just visible, some lying, and others kneeling. Beyond, the horses made uneasy sounds against their hobbles.

Dooley and Lou walked towards the fire, where Alford Cropper was crouched beside a body. He looked up, but didn't speak. Lou kneeled down to look at the body that was rolled into a blanket.

'Oh no,' he groaned, and stared tragically at Alford. He took off his Stetson, and ran a hand over his bruised face. 'I'm sorry, Alford. I really didn't know they'd killed him.'

Alford spoke without looking up. 'He was fourteen years old. That's some age, ain't it,' he added bitterly.

Lou didn't know who to vent his frustration and anger on. He'd told them, a cold camp.

That meant *no fire*. It could have been their mistake. He didn't say anything; it just evened out the mess-up.

After a few uneasy moments, Alford looked to Lou. He was shaken, drained of emotion.

'That's two o' my boys now,' he said. 'When do we ride?'

There was another difficult silence. Then Dooley stepped up between the two men.

'We know they're one less, Alford. Lou shot one of their riders, less than two hours ago,' he told him. Alford grunted and gave Lou an unhappy glare.

Lou moved away to see Ben Finch, who was sitting with his back to a yucca. Beside him sat Barton and Preston, both staring towards the guttering fire. He mumbled some words of understanding, but they didn't respond. They'd just lost another brother, and Lou accepted that.

Ben had a leg wound. He'd cut through his chaps, and Lou saw a neck cloth, bound tight.

'It's no more'n a graze,' Ben said, when Lou asked him about it. 'Ain't gonna slow me down.' Then he asked, 'What do we do now?'

Lou knew it was time for him to make a decision,

and he spoke fast and clear.

'The odds on us comin' out o' this in one piece ain't goin' to get any better. There's not a lot of time, an' if we're goin' to move it'll have to be fast. What do you say?'

'I've told you,' Dooley said. 'Whatever it takes. We're together.'

Lou nodded. 'An' I told *you*. We're in the deep tules. Org Chimm's ridin' from Toya Bend. He's comin' with a posse. If they meet up with Games, that'll more than likely double their numbers, and they'll be ready for us.'

'It'll be difficult to surprise 'em out here,' Rex Newton said.

'Not if we go for Chimm *now*. An' there's ways of usin' the land. But we have to move fast.'

'What about the herd?' asked Ben. 'They'll have moved right up to the border, maybe even crossed it.'

'If we wait until Chimm joins up, you're right. But it'll take the herd more'n a day to make Oklahoma, maybe longer. If we go for Chimm early enough, we can still catch 'em.'

Alford raised himself from beside the body of Stockton. He looked keenly at Lou.

'I'll bury my son. Then we move,' he said, determinedly.

Before early light spilled from the east, they were many miles south. Lou hardly blinked as he stared across the plateau. He'd sat unmoving for hours. It was bitterly cold but Lou felt icy rivers of sweat running down his neck and across his shoulders. The silence and scope of the open range was overpowering, and his heart thumped fast.

The night before, Alford and his boys had scraped a shallow grave for Stockton. To keep off coyotes they'd shaped a mound of dogwood and small stones. Without anything being said, they'd all felt it wasn't much of a last resting place.

But Lou was now occupied with the present. He had to find Chimm, who was somewhere out on the plateau. He'd spot him all right, but there wasn't going to be a best time. The only certainty was that they were there, somewhere.

Another hour on, and a faint whiff drifted towards him, as a low desert breeze suddenly curled downwind. It was the thin reek of woodsmoke, but Lou didn't move. The Chimm camp was closer than he'd thought, which vindicated his stealthy patience.

He peered into the shaddowless landscape, tracing a line of shrub along a dry creek. He spotted the camp as pale, wintry colour broke from the eastern horizon.

Low against the skyline, Lou made his way back to camp. The men gathered around him, anxious, and fixed on action.

'They're a mile off, camped alongside a creek. I couldn't make out a guard, but it ain't goin' to be no turkey-shoot.' Lou looked at the tight faces around him. 'We'll hit 'em hard and fast, it's the only way.'

'We have the advantage of surprise,' Alford said.

'Yeah, that's right, Alford, but we have to ride away again,' Lou said, trying to gauge Alford's state of mind. 'We'll *all* have a job to do when we come back for the herd, remember.' Then he turned to Ben Finch.

'Ben, you know horses. It'll be up to you and Rex to take care of 'em. Run 'em off when you hear the first shots.'

'Yeah, but they'll be tied in, or hobbled.'

'Preston'll take care of that. He too knows about horses,' Alford offered.

Preston nodded confidently, and Lou smiled.

'Good,' he said, and looked at Dooley Ricksen. 'Now, let's all get clear about what we're doin'.'

Within minutes, Lou led them to a bend in the dry-bed creek. It was less than a quarter mile from Chimm's camp. Keeping low, they made their way in silence to within fifty yards of the unsuspecting, still-sleeping men.

Lou held up, and signalled for all to dismount. The men climbed quietly from their horses, secured them to the shrub roots that snagged the shallow banks. Lou drew his Colt, and instinctively checked for a full chamber. He eased back the hammer, took a last look behind him and moved towards Chimm's posse.

18

SOME DOWN

Dawn was beaking as Lou tracked quietly through the brush. He was looking for a night guard, taking no chance on there not being one. From ahead of him, a chuckbird peeped, then scuttled bankside to the creek. He'd found the guard.

The man was stamping his feet, and gasping into the chill air. Lou recognized him at once. It was Lem Brockway, the outlaw from Del Rio. The man who'd snatched the shotgun from Tess on the stoop at Pasadera. The man who'd been told to walk thirty miles to Toya Bend with Loomis Kraal.

It was only then that Lou was sure of its being the Chimm camp, and he felt the touch of cold nerve along his gun arm. He watched the man closely, assessing the character and situation. He remembered Dooley saying, *Not the sort of man you'd want to take home with you.*

From way back along the creek, Lou heard the soft snicker of one of their horses. Brockway heard it too, and raised his hat against the skyline. Lou wondered if the man could see anything from the higher ground and turned around, but all he could see was the dry creek bed. When he turned back Brockway had gone: vanished into the brush between the horses and campsite.

Lou swore, and rammed the heel of his hand and his gun butt into the side of the creek bed. He'd depended on surprise to help square the odds, but suddenly they'd moved on. He swore again; and with his mind made up for him, he fired once in the air, and broke out after Brockway.

By the time Brockway reached campside, men were already crawling from their blankets. Herran Stiles was first out, turning the cylinder of his pistol. Walter Henn rolled on to his knees and pulled himself up by the loose rein of his horse. He was a long-time badlands campaigner, and never hobbled or tethered his mount into line.

Brockway shouted into Org Chimm's ear. The man's response was slow but sure. He got to his feet and looking around him, stretched. 'Did you see 'em?' he asked Brockway.

'I've seen the horses. They're real close, along the creek bed.'

'What the hell's happenin'?' croaked Brewster Zube.

'Don't know yet,' Brockway yelled back. 'But they're close enough to know we're here.'

Henn was pulling on the belly girdle of his saddle. He looked across at Chimm. 'Rangers,' he suggested.

All Chimm's posse had their reasons for being panicked by the Texas Rangers. With night-stiffened arms and legs they kicked from their bedding, grabbed for boots and guns.

Chimm rammed his hat on his head and shouted:

'Where in hell's name they comin' from, Lem?'

Brockway was going to point out where, but he was staring at the figure of Lou Hollister, who was behind Chimm, so instead he made a grab for his gun. He fired, yelling at the same time, and Chimm threw himself sideways as the blast from two guns roared in his ears.

But Brockway had been hit, and Lou was ready to fire again. Brockway caught another bullet, and the pain spilled from his eyes. He was attempting to twist down, to squeeze the agony from low in his belly. His legs lost control, and as he died, he stepped help-lessly forward into the ashes of the camp-fire.

The camp erupted with unnerved men shouting and cursing. At the same time a withering hail of rifle fire swept the camp. Lou crouched low for a few seconds, holding both hands tight against his ears. Judging by the noise, Chimm's posse were emptying their guns.

Chimm himself fired three of four times towards Lou. Lou crooked his left arm over his head and raised his eyes. He saw a man lurch between himself and Chimm, only to be crushed by the cross-fired bullets of Dooley Ricksen and Brewster Zube. He watched, fascinated, as the man cried out, hit the ground still running.

Chimm fired again, but the hammer of his pistol

clinked against the spent cylinder. He threw a glance in Lou's direction and mouthed a few words. Then he turned his back on the uproar.

Lou brought his Colt to bear on the middle of Chimm's back. He thought of his brother, Tench, his father and the Cropper boys. But he bit his lip and let Org Chimm make a run for it.

Herran Stiles, Chimm's top hand, had already made it away, along with one or two others. They'd run for cover, were the ones who'd seen too much to stand and make a fight of it.

Brewster Zube was made of more dogged stuff. With a big Army revolver in his hand, he was staggering backwards, then forwards, as bullets smacked into his body. He tried to yell, but blood surged from his mouth and choked the cry. He raised his gun, firing into the ground ahead of him, then threw it down in disgust. He opened his mouth again, and the sound was rough and gargly as more Cropper bullets finally hacked him down.

Lou took a long, deep breath, and stepped out on to clearer ground when Walter Henn became a silhouette. He pulled back the hammer of his Colt, and in cold anger pulled the trigger. As Henn's horse went down he knew he hadn't made a clean hit. He swore as the man rolled from the saddle and scrambled to his feet to avoid the thrashing forelegs of his stricken mount.

Henn pulled his gun and looked wildly around. But Lou had fired again. The second bullet bent Henn double, then he twisted and fell dead within clawing distance of his horse.

There was no more shooting then, only the after-math of pressing silence. Veils of acrid powder smoke curled slowly across the cold ground, and all Lou could hear was the blunt rumble of running horses. He knew it was Ben Finch and Rex Newton running off Chimm's remuda.

He held his Colt down at his side, and looked back into the brush, at the nearest touch of the creek.

'That's it,' he shouted. 'We've done enough. It's over. Move back to the horses.'

He waited awhile, moving among the bodies of the four men, poking at their guns with the toe of his boot. Then he hunkered down and reloaded his Colt. He took a last cynical look, before making his way back along the edge of the creek.

Alford Cropper was talking to Barton, and Lou made a meaningful nod in their direction. He didn't think words were needed. The men mounted their horses, separating out across the range.

Lou rode fast along the line of the creek, not stop-ping until he was at least a mile from Chimm's shat-tered camp. He was out of range of any remaining guns, but he waited tensely for Ben Finch to get there with the horses. Within minutes he saw Preston Cropper and Rex Newton leading them in.

'It'll come close to thievin' if you take 'em all,' Dooley suggested from beside Lou.

'We'll keep those that belong to us,' Lou replied. 'The others can have a run on the plateau.' He looked at Finch and Cropper. 'Drive 'em way off. We don't want 'em back with Chimm. In the meantime we've got ourselves some rested mounts.'

From twelve hours of night-riding and the fight, Lou and his men were as bushed as their own horses. Yet they were eager, and ready to go on.

With Rex Newton and Preston, Ben brought up the horses, the bloodied neck scarf showing through his ripped chaps. He grinned through the crust of dirt and stubble on his face.

'I got me a mustang back,' he said. 'There's some unbroken Croppers, an' a bunch o' Pasadera. Near thirty in all.'

Dooley laughed. 'The bootmaker's goin' to make a tidy profit from all them feet trudgin' into town.'

'Yeah, it's an "ill wind" sure enough,' Lou said. 'Change your saddles boys. You know what's next, an' we've a journey ahead.'

There was a forty- or fifty-mile ride ahead of them, and through the best part of the night. Games would have been warned of their approach, and Lou grimly considered the fight when they caught up. He knew they'd all be near to breakdown with tiredness, and the horses would be suffering after the long ride.

Lou tugged firmly on the cinch of his fresh mount. If they failed to take the herd, there'd be no outrunning the pursuers. West of the plateau, the only place to hide would be land cracks and gopher holes.

19

WALKING THE PLATEAU

It was approaching first light and for a short while Dooley Ricksen stood off from the herd. He was listening to the night sounds before cutting a route through the bed-grounded longhorns. Careful not to spook the cattle, he rode through the herd, closer to one of Walter Games's night riders.

In the dark isolation, he edged his horse in close to the cowboy. He called softly above the contented lowing:

'Hey, mister, what's your name?'

The man was edgy, and without thinking answered simply, 'Branca.'

Dooley smiled sharply. 'You should have stayed abed, Branca. This ain't the best night to be abroad. Listen to me well.'

The man Branca seemed to accept the problem he was facing, and sat his horse quietly as Dooley explained what was expected of him.

'The border's about forty miles south-east o' here. Ride for it now, 'cause there'll be no welcome back at your camp. You'll be dead before you dismount.'

Dooley whistled gently through his teeth as the rider turned his horse smartly towards the Texas border. He sat for another minute or two, before cantering around the flank of the herd.

When he made out what he was looking for, he veered away from the cattle for fifty yards; then, with his hand on his gun, he slammed his mount's flanks hard into another of Games's riders.

The man's senses had been numbed by tiredness when the dramatic attack on his pony came. He was jerked into a frightened response.

'What the . . . what's goin' . . . who the . . . ?'

Dooley gripped the butt of his gun.

'You're goin' home. I've just sent Branca packin'. You know him?'

The man thought for a second, then made a vain grab for his gun. He fumbled while trying to control his frightened pony.

Dooley drew his own gun, casually leaned over, and lashed out at the cowboy's face. There was a dull moan, and as the man fell sideways his boot-heel caught in the stirrup. The pony snorted, and leaped forward in a blind panic.

Dooley grimaced as the cowboy was dragged face down in the soil. Brutal, but better than being dead, Dooley thought.

Hew Cheddon, the third night rider, had already

made the ten-minute ride back to his camp. He wearily swung a leg from his saddle, and his boot had just touched ground when the long barrel of a .44 Colt stabbed him rudely in the small of his back. The man stiffened as he felt his gun being lifted from his holster.

'Nice an' easy, cowboy,' Lou said.

'Who the hell are you?' the man responded.

'The man who's takin' his herd back.' Lou moved the man away from his horse, prodding him towards the chuck wagon. 'Don't make a fuss, an' you'll live. Come an' meet some o' your friends.'

The camp-fire threw up remaining flickers, and beyond it there was a group of cowhands with tied hands and feet. The Cropper brothers stood guard with rifles.

The man offered his hands to Rex Newton, and then sat down for his boots to be tethered. His colleagues stayed tight-mouthed and sullen.

Dooley Ricksen rode in. Lou walked quickly over to him. He held the snaffle of Dooley's horse.

'How's the the herd? They quiet?' he asked eagerly.

'Yeah, they're quiet. I saw the night crew off without any trouble. They'll be way gone by now. Them longhorns can still be spooked though, most of 'em are half wild.'

Lou was still worried. 'We'll take a chance they can look after 'emselves for another hour or so.'

He turned to Hooper Crewle, the only Games man who wasn't hogtied.

'Your job's to get some breakfast goin'.'

'Wasn't expectin' guests at this hour,' grumbled Crewle. 'Fire's down anyways.'

'Then get it started, or I'll do it myself an' roast you over it,' Lou snapped.

He narrowed his eyes as Crewle kicked tetchily at the dying embers.

Lou tipped a match to the chuck wagon lamp. As the light swelled he rounded on the sitting prisoners.

'Which of you's Walter Games?'

A tanned, sinewy, man with droopy moustaches met Lou's eyes.

'I'm Games,' he said. 'An' you'll be Hollister, no doubt?' he asked with insolent curiosity.

'That's right, an' I own most of this herd you're drivin'. If it means anythin', I've a letter to prove it.'

'Letters ain't exactly my strong suit, cowboy. Word is, you're a killer an' a thief who's on the run. That herd's about as much yours as mine.'

'Only some o' that's right, Games. But just look at it from my point o' view. While you're thinkin' up an excuse for Tusk Tenbridge, I'll be drivin' the herd. It's beef for market, an' I'll be takin' payment in Cuidad Blanco.'

'You'll never see the railhead, Hollister,' Games said.

Lou grinned. 'Oh, I forgot to mention it, but Henn and Zube are crossin' the Styx. An' Chimm? Well, he's forty miles back, walkin' the plateau.'

Games's jaw dropped, and the confident sneer left his face. His men looked at him suspiciously as the meaning sank in.

'That's right, fellas,' Lou picked up. 'Your future's

run dry. The only thing that'll beat us into Cuidad Blanco is daybreak.'

As he spoke, Crewle was emptying the chuckbox of foodstuffs. He looked down at Games, but Lou caught the slyness and turned to Dooley Ricksen.

'Dooley, have a rummage in the wagon. There's probably a shotgun in with his spoons,' he said. Wearily, he looked at Games. 'I'll leave you with your lives. It's more than Tenbridge or Chimm ever would.'

While Lou spooned up beans he considered their next move. Not having slept for forty-eight hours, they were all exhausted, and they'd rode a fair piece. The horses were run in too, but could be replaced with the herd remuda.

'Preston,' Lou said, 'when you're finished, you and your brother get those cowboys into the chuck wagon. Take 'em east into the plateau. Unload 'em, but bring the horses back.'

Dooley helped the boys, and Ben Finch pushed two saddles under the seat of the wagon.

Alford Cropper walked towards his son, Preston.

'Tell 'em,' he said, sternly.

Preston levered a shell into the breech of his rifle and looked arrogantly at the tied-up cowboys.

'If anyone moves, they get out an' walk. It'll be a long way to safety, roped up, an' with a bullet in the middle o'your back.'

Alford looked at Lou, who returned the amused expression. Lou shouted: 'Catch us up,' as Preston and Barton rode off in the wagon.

Lou wondered whether it was something he

should be doing himself, but he had to organize their moving-out to Cuidad Blanco. He wanted to get there fast, but didn't want to race the herd. Every head would lose weight, and that meant money. He needed the greenbacks. Then he'd have *two* ways of unsaddling Tusk Tenbridge.

17

THE LAWMEN

'That ain't my kind o' perfume,' Dooley Ricksen said. They were on a low rise, two miles out of Cuidad Blanco. He inhaled deeply. 'Hell, Lou, but it's still somethin' to savour.'

The town lay before them, a ripe cow-cauldron of animal pens and rough-timbered buildings. The rail station settled the end of the line that ran 150 miles north through Texas before branching east. On either side of the track, ten of the fifty pens held cattle for the slaughterhouses of Kansas City.

For five days they'd moved the herd at a fair pace and without incident. They'd eaten, but not well. Bandannas were pinched tight around their noses, dust shrouded them, and sweat caked the creases of their skin. Crude and rough as it looked, the men were glad to see the town. All except Lou, who was mindful of his return.

Alford Cropper rode stiffly up beside him.

'We go home now?' he grated.

Lou gave him a friendly look. 'If I get paid. I don't want to raise any curiosity, so I'll ride in alone. If it works out, we'll get clear before sundown.'

Dooley rode between them. 'Yeah, that means you stayin' away from that Nathan's Gap doghole.'

Lou twitched his reins, and grinned wryly.

'I'm done with lone drinkin', Dooley. See yah.' He set his Stetson, and gently spurred his horse.

Lou found a buyer at the bar of Dutchman's Hotel. A small, dapper man introduced himself as B.B. Booke, of the Kansas Meat Company. Booke accepted Lou's attestation as legal owner, and agreed to value and buy the whole herd. He immediately went to arrange space in the pens, and Lou returned to his campsite.

Later in the afternoon the cattle were marked down and penned near the railhead, ready for loading into the cars. Booke organized a banker's draft for $10,000, and recommended a buyer for the horses. The few without familiar brands Ben had turned loose along the plateau. The remainder tallied twenty-five head, and Ben sold them to the town's army horsetrader.

Lou deposited the banker's draft at the State Cattlemen's Bank. He paid in to the credit of Clewson Hollister, and drew $2,000 in cash. Out of that, he'd pay Alford, Ben Finch and Rex Newton.

'Stay away from the west side of town, Mr Hollister. They'll kill for a stogie,' the clerk advised.

'I don't smoke,' Lou said, 'but thanks.'

It was sound advice. The cow town was popularly known as 'Blanco Muerte', and had earned it. Lou stuffed his hands deep into pockets and stepped on to the sidewalk. Thugs and gunmen were one thing, Tusk Tenbridge and the law was another. If word was out he was wanted in Texas, it could rouse the interest of a bounty hunter. The boys had gone to Dutchman's Hotel to wait for him. They could take a shave or a bath, maybe have a proper meal and a drink. But they weren't going to stay around long after nightfall.

He walked along to the hotel where he'd left his horse tied-in alongside the others. From the look of the mounts it was obvious they'd recently done some hard travelling, and it provoked the interest of two men who were looking at Lou's chestnut gelding.

As he stepped up to the hitching rail, Lou felt the prickly run of sweat. The men turned casually towards him, their faces expressionless. They both wore long cotton dusters and dark, sweat-stained hats. One said in a toneless voice:

'Evenin'. This your horse, mister?'

Lou's gut tightened as he sensed the unmistakeable, heavy presence of state lawmen. It was what he'd feared. He swallowed hard, and rode it out.

'It is,' he said firmly. 'If it's any o' your business.'

The man raised his eyebrows fractionally and looked towards his colleague.

'You recall him bein' one of 'em?' he asked him.

The second man levelled his gaze at Lou.

'It was back in early summer,' he said. 'I don't recall him bein' with 'em then.'

Lou's nerves were jangling. He turned on both men.

'You got somethin' to say, mister, say it, or let me be.'

'Don't bite just yet, friend,' said the first man. 'I'm Barney Ossler, County Sheriff. We've some questions need answerin'.'

Again Lou looked at both men.

'What questions?'

'I see you're Pasadera. That's Texas. I'd like to know your name.'

'Lou Hollister. An' Pasadera's my father's ranch. I'm carryin' his note.'

Ossler sniffed at Lou's response. He didn't seem too interested one way or the other, but he held out his hand for the paper. Lou felt alongside the wad of dollars for the handwritten document his father had given him. Ossler stiffened slightly as Lou's hand moved, but the other lawman never flinched as his eyes remained on Lou.

'This ain't the place, Mr Hollister,' Ossler said. 'We'll be more comfortable in my office. Let's go.'

Ossler handed the paper to his colleague and indicated for Lou to move along the street. The lawman escorted Lou to his office, which was sandwiched between the mail rider's depot and the livery stable. It was now early evening, and a lamp was throwing its oily, yellow glow across a cluttered desk.

The sheriff took back the paper from his colleague and had a closer look.

'Seems genuine enough,' he said, and returned it to Lou. 'This here's Dashell Tyme,' he continued. 'Deputy marshal, out of Lawton. He's got an interest in your Pasadera ranch.'

Tyme's cold dark eyes met Lou's.

'Pasadera drove a herd up here earlier in the year,' he said flatly.

'You tellin' or askin?' Lou stared back at the deputy marshal, noted the man's steely manner.

Tyme gave a small, twisted smile.

'It's not the herd I'm interested in, Hollister. It's three of the men who came with it. One of 'em was ridin' that chestnut geldin' you say's yours.'

Lou made a twisted smile in return.

'Yeah, that would have been Tusk Tenbridge, he's the sheriff o' Toya Bend. A big man, bald head, wears black. I'm guessin' that Org Chimm, an' a young, scar-faced Mexican were the other two.'

Tyme paused. 'Sounds like 'em,' he said. 'They still ridin' for you?'

'They never rode for *me*, they rode for 'emselves,' Lou cracked back. 'Herido Ochenta, the Mex, is dead, and Chimm's walkin' the desert. For all I know, Tenbridge's still plunderin' Cottonwood County. What's your interest in 'em, Marshal?'

'Murder's top o' the list. They shot a farmer and his family, took their livestock.'

'How'd you know it was them?' Lou asked.

'Took a while for the farmer's wife to die. She talked enough to make it certain. I'd already seen 'em here in town a few weeks before. They're the sort you don't forget.'

'An' Tenbridge was one of 'em?' Lou asked doubtfully.

Tyme shrugged 'As good as. We're certain o' the other two.'

Lou's mind started to race. He was on the run from a lawman who was implicated in murder, and wanted by the federal authority.

'You say these men were never workin' for you?' Tyme stopped Lou's thoughts with his query.

'That's right, Marshal. I've been away a long time. I never knew what was goin' on at Pasadera, but found it in a real wretched state. My father ain't copin' any more. That's where Tusk Tenbridge comes in. He thinks bein' sheriff entitles him to take everythin' that ain't hogtied. That includes my father's ranch.'

Ossler was shuffling some papers on his desk.

'Let me guess,' he drawled. 'That Mexican you say's dead, and Chimm. You caught up with 'em?'

Ossler exchanged an amused glance with Tyme, and Lou sensed maybe there was some understanding between them.

'With your permission, Sheriff, I need to get back to Toya Bend and the ranch,' he said.

Ossler nodded. 'I'm satisfied, an' Texas is way beyond my jurisdiction. But remember there's a telegraph, and Dashell here's federal. You'll be getting yourselves a new state governor down there next year. Tenbridge and that free-loadin' rabble have had their run.'

As he walked from the sheriff's office towards Dutchman's Hotel, Lou twinged from the uncanny sensation of a bullet in the middle of his back. He understood Ossler's warning about Tenbridge, knew that next year was going to be just a few months too far.

21

MURDER

Slumped, big-shouldered in his chair, Tusk Tenbridge glowered through the window at the cheerless street. It was mid-afternoon and the cold was invasive. From where he sat he couldn't see the lone horesman who rode slowly through the cotton-woods at the edge of town.

Herran Stiles and Loomis Kraal were time-killing. They sat at a small table playing penny-ante with Org Chimm. Domus Kraal lay on a cot, his hat pulled over his begrimed face. Loomis made a nasal snigger as he clawed a pile of small coins towards him. Chimm twitched irritably.

Without taking his eyes off the deserted street, Tenbridge grumbled:

'Hollister knew where you were. How'd he know that?'

'For God's sake, Tusk, I didn't hang around to ask. How many more times I got to tell it? Stiles saw their horses, then they just came out o' the creek bed, guns blazin'.'

Chimm was still ornery from his crippling trek back from the plateau. His eyes carried their hurting look, and Tenbridge's constant badgering wearied and bored him. Stiles kept silent, but he too was chafing to get even.

Making a column of his coins, Loomis smirked.

'You ain't even got enough for sherbet dabs now, Org.'

As the squawk of his voice hung in the air, Chimm gave a look that chilled the ooze on Loomis's chin.

From taking off into the Edwards Plateau, Chimm had met up with Stiles and three others. Together they'd walked near ten miles before meeting a prospector. The old man had two mules that he'd led down from the Sacramentos. One of the cowboys handed over five dollars for Chimm and Stiles to take a mule each.

Tenbridge had heard nothing from Games; had no idea of what had happened to the herd. He was still wondering if they'd made it to Ciuidad Blanco when he noticed the man riding towards his office.

'Looks like we've got a visitor,' he said. Domus Kraal pushed his hat away from his face.

The rider had dismounted and tethered his big bay horse to the hitch rail. Tenbridge twisted in his chair, buckled on his gunbelt as the man paused to shake out his duster. Against the last of the day's light, the man's shadow fell through the open doorway. He stopped to pin on a silver badge, and as he entered the office Tenbridge saw the set of confidence and hard purpose.

'Well, it's been a while since a US marshal paid us a visit,' Tenbridge said without getting up. 'Must be somethin' of real import.'

The man looked around the sheriff's office. He looked hard at Chimm, then concentrated on Tenbridge.

'I'm Dashell Tyme, Deputy US Marshal. I carry warrants for three men. Two I can use.'

Tenbridge moved around in his chair; instinct made him careful.

'You have names or descriptions, Marshal?'

'Oh sure,' Tyme confirmed, sweeping up a shotgun from beneath his long duster. The action was smooth and fast. 'Big man, bald head, wears black. That tells me it's you, Sheriff.' Tyme nodded in the direction of Chimm. 'An' this mean-lookin' one with the long hair's Org Chimm.'

'You reckon you're goin' to serve them warrants, Marshal?' Chimm hissed.

'I'm here to try, mister.' With his thumb, Tyme eased back the twin hammers. Flicking his gaze from Tenbridge to Chimm, he spoke to Domus Kraal. 'You on the cot. If you want to stay breathin', get back to sleep.'

Kraal puffed, and nestled his hat back into his mattress of beard.

Chimm said to the marshal. 'What are them warrants for?'

'Murder. Farmers on the border. It was a big mistake in leavin' the lady alive.'

Tenbridge pushed himself away from his desk, hands held in front of him.

'Hell, Marshal, none of us been near any goddamn border.'

'Keep still, kid,' the marshal snapped as Loomis made to get out from the table. Then he said to Tenbridge, 'You was there. You an' the palomino sort there, Chimm. Ochenta was the Mexican. There's others in Cuidad Blanco to testify to that.'

Time was running out and all those in the room knew it. Domus Kraal hadn't moved, the only sound was the heavy rattle of his breathing.

Loomis was smiling in callow foolishness, but he knew his father was up to something. With his finger-tip, he pushed at the column of coins until it collapsed across the table. A few pennies chinked to the floor, and the tension broke. For an instant, Dashell Tyme's attention wavered.

The concussion from the shotgun thundered around the walls of the room and slammed against the ceiling. Dashell Tyme sucked in his breath and held it, his face becoming a garish, swollen mask. His head bent forward as if trying to see the enormous blade of the Bowie knife that protruded from low in his throat.

The marshal choked and gargled as he staggered forward, but Stiles had leaped from the table, and was on him. He yanked at the shotgun and, as Tyme fell, he pushed him sideways away from the door. He watched as bright blood crept across the marshal's duster, then turned to Chimm.

'Well done, Org, you just killed yourself a US marshal.'

Tusk Tenbridge sat immobile in his chair, sweat glistening across his broad face.

'Christ, Org, how the hell do we get out o' this?' he breathed aghast.

'You're the sheriff, Tusk. Arrest somebody.'

Loomis Kraal had a wild attack of sniggering, and Domus Kraal rolled off the cot and stood up. He wiped a paw across his hairy face.

'Hell of a place to try an' get some sleep. You've all jus' woke up most o' Boot Hill.'

Astonished, Loomis jigged over to the marshal. As he bent to retrieve Stiles's knife, Domus shouted:

'Leave it, Loomis, there's enough of a mess already.'

Tenbridge was staring out into the street, waiting for the first signs of interest. He was thinking as fast as he could, and trying to gain some composure.

'Shouldn't be any problem for a while,' he said.

Herran Stiles's eyes narrowed, and he looked at Tenbridge doubtfully.

'For a while?' he echoed. 'I reckon your time as sheriff's already run out, Tusk.'

Chimm joined in with his own thoughts.

'Yeah, Tusk. I'm tirin' o' this whole business. We ain't got anythin' yet. When Tyme don't turn up, there'll be a whole bunch o' big lawmen down here, and Hollister's still out there somewhere. There's big trouble for us all, *right now.*'

Tenbridge grunted, staring uncertainly at the body of Tyme.

'Pull him into the back room, Loomis. After dark, take him out a few miles.'

Domus Kraal was looking out at the marshal's bay mount.

'You goin' to ride his horse, Tusk? It's sure big enough.'

Loomis poked his head out through the door.

'I'll take 'em both, but what we goin' to do then?'

Chimm looked from Stiles to Tenbridge.

'I say we ride to Pasadera. You've unfinished business there, Tusk.'

Tenbridge watched as Loomis dragged Tyme across the puncheoned floor.

'That's right. I'll get somethin' out o' this mess.'

'You'll be thinkin' o' that girl, Tusk?' Domus Kraal cackled.

'Yeah, and the Hollister boy. He'll turn up sooner or later. You're right, Org. We've made nothin' so far, might as well get some satisfaction.'

'That's your way, Tusk. Just don't forget the ruckus you started by mouthin' off about that girl's bloodline. There's folk around here once looked up to the Hollister family. If there's any shame, they'll want to make it 'emselves.'

'Let 'em, then.' Tenbridge slammed his Stetson back on his gleaming bald head. 'Seems it's all a bit late to go worryin' about what the folk round here think.'

22

THE RETURN

Four days after leaving Cuidad Blanco, Lou Hollister's outfit was back through Palo Duro Canyon. They continued south, discreet and vigilant, over the hard, grinding land. They were outlawed in Texas, and strangers brought the risk of trouble. But they saw no one, and no one saw them.

Lou rode well up front. With the skill of a mail rider he used the natural shape of the land to give himself cover. For ten more days they travelled, making use of hollows and dried-out gullies. It was when they were camped along an upper reach of the Pecos, with its rising water, that Lou had the premonition. It was a gut sensation of impending grief for Pasadera.

It took them five more days to reach the low bluff that overlooked the ranch. Lou reined in and scanned ahead. It was approaching midday, and the sun had decided against showing itself. From where he sat, the ranch house was too distant to be made out clearly; its adobe whiteness almost glowing in the cold colours of the land. From across the peaks of the Sacramentos grey snow-clouds had formed, and Lou watched the heavy sky as it spread eastwards. Waiting patiently while the others rode into file alongside him, he wondered how long before the snow fell.

'I'll go in alone from the east, Dooley,' he said. 'You and the others come in from the west.' The mood was telling, but nobody queried their purpose.

Tense and unstrung, Lou heeled the gelding into a canter. After a few minutes he stopped to watch a plume of dark smoke coil its way upwards. The icy grip of fear returned to the pit of his stomach.

He kicked the horse into a gallop, making for the tangles of mesquite that pitted the land near the house. It was near reckless flight, and Lou paid scant attention to the likelihood of ambush. He leapt from the saddle and ran forward with the horse. There was no sign of life, only the strong, drifting smell of burning. He turned upwind, and from the edge of the yard he stared, numbed, at the ranch house.

Around the doorway and windows the adobe walls were sooted black. Most of the roof was gone, charred beams angled into the sky. The stone chimney rose from the pile of smouldering tiles where the roof had fallen in. He pulled his horse forward, his Colt gripped in his right hand.

He stood beside the corral rails and stared at the beaten-up ground where horses had panicked to get out. The broken corpse of one small cowpony lay in the yard, its limbs stretched taut. For a full minute he listened, but there was no sound other than the crackle of searing wood. He looked at the blackened, smoking ruin that had once been his home.

In the gap between the doorposts, his father's lap-rug was wrapped around the wheel of his toppled chair. His gaze wandered, noting detail with cold anger. The stoop was littered with pots, dishes and household things, all smashed to rubble before being burned.

He stood, horrified. What had happened to his father and Teresa? Where were they? The reins dropped from his fingers and he took a step towards the porch. Family possessions had been piled in the middle of the front room and torched. The kitchen and back bedrooms weren't badly damaged, and he turned to see that the barn and outbuildings were untouched. He stooped, ran a finger around the rim of a hoof print, and looked hard into the distance.

He heard the sound from off to his left, near a short run of toolsheds. He rolled forward into the ground, turning on his side, his arm outstretched, the Colt steady in his hand.

'Get out here,' he bellowed. 'Get into the open, or I'll come find you'. He raised himself on one knee and gripped the Colt with both hands. His voice dropped, contorted with rage. 'Believe me, you'll die real painful.'

'Don't shoot, Lou. Please, don't shoot.' From a tight gap between two sheds, Tess reeled into the yard. She fell to her knees, ashen, every nerve and sinew dragging her down.

'Tess,' Lou yelled, running towards her. 'Where is everybody? Where's my father?'

Tess clawed her fingers across her smeared, swollen face, and Lou, crouching before her, laid his gun on the ground.

'I'm sorry, are you hurt?' he asked, anxiously.

She shook her head wretchedly, and fought for the words.

'No, I'm all right . . . It's your father . . .' She held up a trembling arm. 'I think he's in there ... I think they killed him, Lou.'

Tess's voice beat around Lou's head as he ran, oblivious to the lacerating claws of the mesquite. The body lay across the exposed roots of a gnarled cottonwood, and Lou's breath was rasping as he looked down on the fuzzed, gaunt face of his father. The old man's eyes were closed, and his skin was thin and limpid. It was almost the face of a stranger, except for the long nose and hostile clench of his jaw. Lou took a few deep breaths, and his heart was thumping. He knelt and placed his fingers gently between where blood had welled then dried in patches across Clewson's broken chest.

That was it. It didn't really matter about anyone else. It would be for his father that men would die. All those responsible for the hardship and torment they'd wreaked upon the old man.

Faltering, and in tears, Tess poured out what had happened.

'It was still dark, very early . . . there were noises from the corral. I thought it was you and Dooley,

come back. But there were more horses in the yard
... I got out of bed to see what was happening. Clew
was there, pulling open the front door . . . I could see
his shotgun in his lap. There were men making so
much noise. Clew shouted, then fired out at them. I
couldn't see anything . . . it was too dark . . . he was in
the doorway.'

Lou looked across at the charred framework of the
door and his father's blanket.

'What happened then? What happened to you?'

'There was lots of shooting . . . bullets came
through the door as well. I hid back in my room.
Clew was hit . . . I heard it . . . the terrible sound. I
could still see through my door. Tusk Tenbridge was
there. I heard his voice. Then they drove off the
horses. One of them came up the steps . . . he
dragged Clew away. I only found him when they'd
gone. I couldn't do anything . . . didn't know what to
do.'

'Yeah, I can imagine,' Lou said, distractedly. He
was already thinking that he'd have to leave the girl
there for a while. She was the best person to tend his
father.

From the corner of his eye he caught the sudden,
uneasy movement of his horse as four riders galloped
across the yard. Dooley Ricksen was leading, his eyes
flashing.

'What the hell, Lou?' He looked unbelievingly at
Tess, then at the burned ranch house. 'Where's the
old man?'

'They killed him. He's in the brush.'

'Who, Tenbridge?'

Lou was trying to throw off his shock.

'Yeah, him or his men. From the look of it, all of 'em.'

Pulling off his hat, Alford Cropper rode his buckskin up close. His jaw was clenched tight, but he was in control.

'Barton will take the lady to Teeside,' he said to Lou. 'He'll send some men back. Preston will stay here and take care of your father's body. I'll ride with you now.'

Lou didn't feel like talk any more. He watched as Preston dismounted to offer up the reins. 'No,' Tess said, 'I'm staying here. It's been my home for a long time now. Besides, there's some livestock left that still needs feeding.' She tried a small smile, and looked up at Alford. 'It would be very kind if you helped me with Clew, but then I'd like to be alone. Go with Preston, then bring some help. There's no one coming back here for a while. What would they want?'

Lou looked at the stunned faces around him.

'You all know where I'm goin'. If you're still with me, Dooley, we'll ride now.'

Without turning back, the two men rode from the yard. They were headed due south, into the approaching snow and Toya Bend.

Half-way to the town, Lou reined up, sharply swinging his horse in a tight circle. He turned to Dooley, and shouted:

'This is all wrong, Dooley. Get back to the ranch. They're goin' to return. Chimm and Stiles, Kraal as well, maybe. It's not the ranch they want any more –

that's why they hadn't any qualms about setting fire to it – it's personal. Look out for Tess, they'll want her too. Meet me out beyond the cottonwoods when I return. Get goin'.'

It was a big, heavy snowfall that moved in from the foothills of the Sacramentos. Lou pulled at his collar and felt behind his saddle for a slicker.

23

FALL OF A LAWMAN

Tusk Tenbridge yawned and stretched himself in his chair. He swung his legs up and propped them on the edge of the desk. He looked at the melt water that trickled down the walls from the warped shakes, and the failed daylight irritated him. He considered going over to see Chester Bumpass for an early snifter. He snatched up his hat and stepped from the office, looked along to the saloon, then across the street. In less than an hour, the hard-packed dirt had become a deep, white carpet. He could just see thin, yellow light set back in Chester's hardware store, and he grinned evilly. He tightened a short scarf and pulled the door to behind him. If Chester had something for a thirst, he'd get his deputy, Mel Pawkson, to look after the town for the rest of the night.

It was full dark when Lou reined in at the north end

of Toya Bend. He dismounted quietly, and hitched his horse to a broken-down rig.

The town seemed to be in hiding, the main street lying bright, silent and empty before him. A light shone outside Toya's Table, but the place wasn't busy, and most of the town's other buildings were in snow-capped darkness.

There was a lamp in the livery barn, and he could see a mule snatching at a hay pile. The blacksmith was whittling, and as Lou approached he gave a slight look of annoyance at being disturbed. Lou was bereft of any nicety, and stepped up quickly beside the man's chair. He grabbed at a heavy, wool vest, and dragged the surprised smith to his feet.

'I don't aim to disturb you for long. I'm lookin' for the sheriff. You'd know if he's in town an' I want to know where he is.'

The man stared at him truculently, but didn't reply. Lou could see the fear in the man's eyes, which flicked to the shotgun resting against an animal cage.

'I just want to know where he is. I can beat it out o' you if I have to.'

'He'll kill me, if he finds out I told you.'

Lou deliberately pulled the Colt from around his waist, and ran the barrel around the base of the blacksmith's jaw.

'That's the *long* game mister. I'll kill you *now* if you don't tell me.'

'Try Chester Bumpass, across from the saloon. That's where he goes most nights.'

Lou's manner was emotionless. He released his hold and stepped back a pace.

'Where's the deputy?'

'He'll be over at the jail.'

Lou cast a quick glance at the shotgun.

'It'd be a real smart move if you carried on with your carvin' for a while.'

The blacksmith dropped back into his chair.

'I wasn't thinkin' of goin' anywhere.'

It was a half-hour later when Tenbridge returned to his office. He locked the door behind him, didn't take off his coat and hat. He was going back to his chair, when Lou Hollister confronted him from the storeroom.

Tenbridge groaned as the muzzle of a Colt .44 stared at his forehead.

'Who was it shot my father?' Lou asked with quiet menace.

The sheriff's eyes bulged with sudden fear as Lou pushed the barrel of his Colt against his stomach.

'Tell me who shot my father,' Lou repeated.

Tenbridge's blood drained from his face.

'That's nothin' to do with me.'

'Everythin' that happens here's to do with you, Tenbridge. Tell me who pulled the trigger, you larded sonofabitch.'

Lou pushed his left hand up tight, under Tenbridge's throat. He gripped, pushing backwards until the big man stumbled awkwardly into his chair. The sheriff was sweating, and shaking uncontrollably.

Lou thumbed back the hammer of the Colt.

'I'll push the barrel in real deep, Sheriff. That way nobody'll hear the bang when I pull the trigger.'

139

'It was Chimm,' Tenbridge gasped.

Lou swore under his breath. He stared at the floor between Tenbridge's boots, then looked around the office. There was a shotgun lying across the top of an empty stove, and a bottle with an inch of whiskey on the table. He picked it up and had a mouthful. The he pushed his Colt back in his waistband and cleaned his hands with the remaining liquid.

He turned his head as if to say something, then back-turned the key in the door lock. He stood for a short while in the doorway, considering. After a moment's silence he heard Tenbridge move, and turned to face him.

The sheriff was standing in the far corner of his office, the shotgun gripped tightly and pointed at Lou.

'You'll be back for me, Hollister, we both know it. I can't let you walk away,' he said, almost tragically.

Lou understood Tenbridge's dilemma and made no reply. He stepped out into the whiteness with nothing but contempt and disgust for the sheriff. It was only when he heard the distinctive click of the shotgun's twin hammers that he turned, his hand scarcely moving inside his gleaming slicker.

Tusk Tenbridge was a grasping opportunist, not a cold-blooded killer, and he didn't fire when he should have. He jerked back as Lou's bullet struck him in the chest. He took the impact with a violent, backwards jerk, then he pitched forward. As his eyes clouded, he didn't even summon up the strength to trigger the shotgun. Lou shuddered at the thought of the man's big, meaty face slamming into the hard floorboards of his own office.

Lou glanced at the body in disbelief, then at the torn hole in the front of his slicker. His top lip twisted cynically.

'Whatever it was you wanted, Sheriff, I wonder if you ever considered dyin' for it.'

He walked quickly back to his horse, and didn't look back.

24

ROUSING TESS

Lou's horse snorted alarm, and he slowed him to a trot. Through the unnerving silence of the snow he heard the footfalls of another horse. He listened for a moment trying to locate a figure. He was disorientated, but decided the sound was coming from the direction of Pasadera ranch. He held his horse in tight and waited, still and silent.

The rider was keeping to the wagon road that trailed back towards Toya Bend. Lou's mare snorted loudly again, and he jerked the reins and made hush noises. But the man on the horse had pulled away from the trail to locate the sound. Through the snow that had brightened with the dawn light, he came close. He saw the blurred shape of Lou, and walked slowly towards him.

'Lou. Lou Hollister,' he called.

Under his slicker, Lou eased forward the hammer of his Colt and pushed the gun back into his waistband.

'You're takin' a chance,' he muttered.

'An you came close to bein' dead.'

He recognized the voice of Dooley Ricksen shouting back.

Dooley hooked his gun back into his holster and edged his mount closer.

'They've come back, Lou. You were right. I decided to ride out and find you. Couldn't tell where the hell I was goin'. Using the trail as a marker, I got away without 'em seein' me, but Tess's still there.'

Lou kneed his horse as it swung around, restless, under the relentless surge of snow. He stared into the bright, hazy range.

'I'll go and get her, then.'

'There's at least four of 'em, Lou. They'll be lookin' out for 'emselves. Just waitin' for you.'

'Tryin' to scare me, Dooley?'

'No. I'm comin' in with you. There'll be nothin' here for me if I don't. Your old man never did any harm to no one. He only ever helped me an' your Scorby,' Dooley said, nodded with conviction.

Lou smiled understandingly. 'Perhaps we've wasted enough time.'

'Yeah,' Dooley said. 'Sometime you can tell me what you did to Tusk Tenbridge.' He threw a doubtful glance at Lou. 'My pa once told me there'd be days like this.'

Teresa stirred slightly, sighed and opened her eyes. As she twisted and glanced about, her memory returned. Six hours before she'd rolled herself into a blanket on her bed. Under the unbroken fall of snow, and out of despair, she'd drifted off to sleep.

She heard sounds from out in front of the house, and swung her legs on to the floor. She recognized the voices of the men who'd brought the burning and death to Pasadera; the voices of men who, she'd thought, had gone.

She drew a leather jerkin and a pair of boots from her wardrobe. From the back of the cupboard she grabbed the Quickloader. She crossed to the window, raised a corner of the drawn blind, and peered out. There was a tinge of dawn-grey creeping in from the east, and the land was filled with white. The snow slanted into the room around her feet as she raised the wooden windowframe.

She crouched beneath the windowsill, and snowflakes feathered in a cold edge across her neck. She couldn't see beyond the livery stable, and decided to try for an annexed tool-shed. She was cold, alone and frightened. Eventually, one of the Kraals or Org Chimm would come looking for her, and the ranch would be searched with a fine-toothed comb.

She levered a shell into the carbine. The ranch was her home, and for the first time, she felt totally alone and vulnerable.

25

REPRISAL

The horses were tethered inside a protective brake of cottonwood where, under the heavy blanket of snow, there was little fear of being seen from the burnt remains of ranch house.

Keeping low, the two men made their way forward. It took them fifteen minutes to reach the edge of the yard. Although daylight had increased, visibility had worsened to less than fifty feet.

Dooley looked suddenly worried, and he'd started to shiver.

'Where do you reckon they are, Lou?'

'Don't know. There'll be one of 'em looking out front, an' another out back, but they'll be under cover.'

Dooley stared gloomily around him, but the snow hashed up all visibility. They couldn't see any of the ranch house buildings.

Lou stared at him hard. 'You can ride away,

Dooley. There ain't nothin' wrong with wantin' to see the end of the day.'

'Nah, I'm stayin'. I'll go back a bit, get around the side of the sheds. D'ya think Tess'll be in the house, Lou?'

'Yeah, I guess so. They'll have her cooped up, somewhere.'

Lou trembled involuntarily then looked up to see Dooley ducking off and away to his left.

Dooley Ricksen steadied his tense muscles. He tunnelled his eyes straight ahead, but relaxed, waiting for the slightest movement to show. Like Lou, he wanted retaliation, and as the tautness ebbed he walked resolutely into the whiteness. There was movement ahead of him, and he swung his pistol to cover, swore at his reflection that fluttered in a cracked window. He sidled over to the wall of a storehouse that spurred from the livery stable. He expected some sort of sign or noise, but nothing moved and he stepped back into the open. He wondered if Tenbridge's men had decided to pull out while there was still time, but doubted it.

Slowly he moved back to the storehouse. The snow was falling thick and heavy, forming an overpowering cushion of silence that had him surrounded. He pondered on Stiles, Org Chimm or the Kraals being hidden in the lee of one of the ranch buildings, ready to shoot him without warning.

He turned his back to the open door, and didn't hear the movement behind him. He just caught a timber creak, then the clack of a shotgun hammer as

146

it fell against an inactive cartridge. His body contracted, half-waiting for the searing red punch, but it didn't happen. He whirled to face Loomis Kraal. The young nit-brain was staring with disbelief at his gun's misfire.

Dooley hurled himself at Loomis. They went down in a heap with legs and arms jerking violently. Dooley felt a sharp pain deep in his side, but gripped his pistol and staggered to his feet. Loomis had dropped the shotgun, and pulled a bloodied skinning-knife. He crouched, gathering himself, but he knew he was beaten. As he leapt, Dooley stretched out his arm and fired.

With a bullet through the centre of his face, Loomis buffered into Dooley as he came forward. With one hand Dooley clutched at the pain in his side as Loomis's arm whirled into him. He staggered into the doorway, feeling the cold agony as the blade sliced deep along his gun arm. The boy who had been about to become a killer lay spread-eagled at his feet. Dooley's breath was grating in spasms, and as his gun fell from his fingers he crumpled into unconsciousness.

With his face pressed into the ground, Dooley didn't understand the point of pressure, low against his spine. It was when he twisted his head, that he grunted in despair. It was all the time he had, before pain exploded and blackness took him again.

Herran Stiles laid his rifle on the ground, and tied Dooley's hands with a strip of rawhide. He made a noise of satisfaction as he jerked the knot tighter, then he straightened up and stood back. He'd pulled the front of Dooley's vest up high, jammed into his mouth to prevent him calling out when his senses returned. Last of all, Stiles dragged Dooley to his feet, and sat him propped against a barrel in the open doorway of the storehouse.

The reverberation of Dooley's gun had flattened Lou into the yard which was already ankle-deep in snow.

The gunshot had to be trouble for Dooley, and Lou made his move. He raised himself quickly, and ran diagonally for a cluster of stores and sheds. They were no more than a featureless barrier, but ahead of him Lou picked out the darker shadow above an open doorway. He couldn't make out a clear picture, only that he seemed to have the advantage of surprise as he bore down on a figure, crouching low.

From behind the cover of Dooley, Herran Stiles fired. The bullet brushed Lou's neck, forcing him sideways, then down on to one knee. By then his Colt had found the indistinct shape of the bloody figure in the doorway, and he pulled the trigger.

Through the falling snow, Lou saw Dooley's face snap up as the bullet hit him, as for a split second, consciousness and feeling returned to his partner.

Lou's eyes blazed with the instant terror of what had happened. He yelled futilely as Dooley was slammed back into the doorway. He beat the Colt against his leg with anger and frustration. But he couldn't undo what he'd done and he made anguished hexes and threats as he backed off. Now he would concentrate on taking out Chimm's men alone.

Stiles had already left the storehouse through a back door. He looked around him, then slithered along the cloudy shadows of the outbuildings, back to the company of Domus Kraal and Org Chimm.

Lou wondered how long it would be before the gunfire brought them out for him. He backed off, looking for a gap between the adobe walls.

Under the charred, partly exposed roof of the ranch house, Domus Kraal and Org Chimm were standing close to the windows that fronted the yard. After the shooting, they were waiting for Herran Stiles to return.

Kraal looked across at Chimm.

'How many shots you heard?'

Chimm turned the cylinder of his Colt, smiling at the sharp clicks it made.

'The same as you. Three,' he said.

'You sure?'

'Yeah, I'm sure.'

'What the hell's happenin' out there? You reckon Hollister's fetched help? Them Croppers maybe? Stiles should have finished him off. You heard my Loomis's shotgun?'

Chimm slipped the Colt in its holster, put the gun belt around his waist and felt the gun's solid weight against his hip.

'No. Don't know who's shootin' who. You'll have to go out there and find out.' He grinned, then laughed. 'I wonder if Hollister's met up with Tusk?

That man ain't come back here to bless us.'

They both knew that Kraal was choking back a fear of being caught plumb between Stiles and Lou Hollister's crossfire.

Chimm was tired of the wait. He grabbed Kraal's Stetson and sugan and threw them to him.

'Fer Chris'sake, Domus, let's go get him.' He saw himself in a cracked, hanging mirror, and adjusted his gun belt. 'I ain't goin' to be out there long enough to become no snow puddin',' he scoffed.

Ahead of Kraal, Chimm grabbed a Winchester and stepped out on to the stoop of the ranchhouse. The ground in front of him had become a vast blanket of white. The snow billowed along the front of the building and brushed his face, but he didn't appear to notice. He was waiting for Kraal to join him.

'What the hell you doin' in there, Domus?' he shouted. 'You afraid o' this stuff, or is it somethin' else?'

Kraal appeared in the doorway.

'I wonna know where the girl is. She's got that carbine, remember?'

The two men stared around, but they couldn't see the livery stable or the adjoining buildings. There was a short, sharp hiss, and then, close in to the front of the charred porch, Stiles edged towards them. He lifted the barrel of his rifle, pointed it in the direction of the worksheds.

26

GUNFIGHT

The heavy grey clouds rolled east, but in twelve hours the snowfall had smothered the land. There was no sound, other than the harsh breathing of fearful men.

Snow was drifting around the outbuildings where Lou was waiting patiently. He knew his only chance was to take all three men on his own terms. He wasn't going to be rushed; he would make gain of the weather and the territory.

From the cover of a fodder pen, he was watching as snowflakes gathered on the drooping brim of Domus Kraal's Stetson. Dragging the battered brim down low, Kraal was waving for Chimm and Stiles to spread. He was carrying a Springfield carbine and a Colt.

Lou edged himself forward, hardly one pace, through the layering snow. He flicked his head sharply from side to side and hefted his Colt, wrapping its lanyard tight around his wrist. He was outnumbered and didn't intend to invite these men to a shooting contest. He brought up the gun and stood sideways on, his body partially hidden by a broken, swinging door.

He watched Stiles as he backed away from Kraal and Chimm and as he stepped into a tub that was lying broken apart in the snow. Stiles cursed and as he jerked at his foot he briefly lost his balance. It was a tough shot, but the chance that Lou needed.

He fired low into the body of Stiles, knowing that at least he'd go down. The man dropped his rifle and clutched his groin. He spat towards Lou, tried to penetrate the snowfall. His foot got twisted, and he fell flat and stretched across the snow-covered staves.

A barrage of lead from Kraal's carbine immediately crashed into the pen, splintering loose planks and fragmenting feed sacks.

Lou slithered sideways along the adobe walls, then made a headlong dash for another shed. As he ran across the open ground, he heard the curious muffled sound of Kraal's warning shout. He glanced over his shoulder, and saw two figures burst out from either side of the barn, and Kraal yelled again.

Kraal was running, pointing backwards towards the sheds, when the bullet took him between the shoulder blades. He stopped, bent low forwards. Then he slowly straightened, staggered back with short staccato steps. He buckled sideways, his big hands making a grab at Org Chimm's gunbelt, then he collapsed, his back a dark, spreading pool of blood.

Chimm shoved himself free, and brought his rifle

to bear on Lou's running figure. Ahead of him, Lou saw a windowframe shatter as he skewed towards the stable. Breath was rasping in his throat, and bullets were tearing into the woodwork ahead of him.

Unsure of who else was out there; unsure of who'd shot Domus Kraal, Lou backed into an open doorway. He listened for the dull crunch of Chimm's feet through the snow, but only heard the plaintive yelp of a coyote through the silence. He blew melt water from the chambers of his Colt. He knew the killer wouldn't follow him into the danger of an outbuilding. Stiles and Kraal were already down, and Chimm wouldn't want to follow suit.

Under cover of dripping overhangs and stacked timbers, Lou worked his way to within fifty feet of the livery stable. Visibility was just that far, and he could make out the grain-gate in the end of the upper storey. Above the stalls was a risky position with no way out, but he could look down. He heard the Winchester roar from close by, and felt a thump above his elbow, then pain as the scorch bruised into his upper arm. He swore, blew a cone of frosted breath.

Chimm, now having marked him, was comparatively safe and more sure of himself. Another bullet clanged and whined off a pump-head that rose near the stable. Lou made his move, and as he ran across the open ground he turned and saw Chimm emerge from between the sheds.

Lou twisted into the livery stable. He jumped on to an empty crate and hauled himself up into the low rafters of the hay loft. The straw was mouldy, and the grain bags were split and rotten. Lou let his Colt hang from his wrist as he levered himself into a sitting position. Awkwardly he shoved one of the heavy bags into a corner of the grain-gate.

Down below, Clewson's old wagon mule stamped nervously in its stall. Lou fell painfully on to his right shoulder and held his Colt tight into his waist. He looked down, and saw two coyote pups dragging on the entrails of a rabbit. He grimaced in revulsion, pointed the long barrel of his Colt down at the insensible animals, and cocked the hammer.

The gun's roar hammered around the stable, and he turned away as fur scraps, and splotches of crimson exploded into the cold slush.

Lou knew that it was only a matter of seconds before Chimm wondered about the noise. Another hail of bullets was the response, and Lou slid back into the pile of straw. Cold sweat ran into his eyes, and he rubbed it away with the crook of his arm. He clambered from the loft, wincing from his wound and the withering fire that immediately poured up through the grain-gate. Hunks of roofing were torn away, and snow swarmed through the tie-beams. The mule was lashing out at the rear of his stall, and its eyes bulged in panic.

Where snow had drifted through the open rear door, Lou stood very still. After a full minute he saw two more pups run for cover, then he made out the blurry figure of Chimm moving from the cover of the sheds. He was staring about him nervously, his hands clutched tightly around the Winchester as he tried to make a fix on the gunshot.

Lou's eyes ached as he watched him, then he couldn't bear the suspense any longer.

'It's the way you'd appreciate, Killer. No chance,' he shouted in mocking desperation.

Chimm was caught in mid-stride as Lou's first bullet hit him high in the chest. He snapped forward as the second broke his rifle and hand at the same time. Sharp bewilderment cracked his face as he stared down at finger bones that were stuck in the trigger guard. With his other hand he stretched for his Colt, then he closed his eyes and went down. He turned over slowly, with crushed snow settled in the hollows of his face. He spat, spluttered something across at Lou, but his pale, empty eyes didn't open again. His boots moved once as they heeled the ground in defeat.

Lou shivered and pushed the Colt back into his waistband, then he walked out into the dead sound. Stiles's poncho was bloated around his neck, and from low down in his body a dark stain soaked slowly into the crushed snow.

Domus Kraal's body was shrouded beneath his heavy, patched sugan. His hat was lying across the top part of his face. His eyes would be staring upward, unseeing, and his mouth was open, filling with the clean, instant-melt of hefty snowflakes.

Lou could have told Dooley that Kraal was at last getting himself a long, cold soak.

In the doorway of a tool-shed, Tess was leaning forward, her face as white as the land. Cold and shocked, she stared out at the bodies, her lips trembling, trying to force a sound. The carbine dropped from her fingers, and it clattered dully off the floor before sinking into the snow. She took a faltering step towards Lou, and he held out an arm.

The snow continued to fall, and Lou understood the watery smudges on Tess's face. The fighting was at an end.

27

AFTERMATH

Since the terrible conflict, Tess and Lou had been living at Teeside. They hadn't spoken much; Tess was troubled with her shooting of Domus Kraal, and for a while Lou had been tormented by his shooting of Dooley Ricksen. It was only for a while though. The bullet from Lou's Colt had wedged itself in the big buckle on Dooley's leather belt. Apart from bruising, it wasn't much of an injury. He was laid up from the knife wounds inflicted by Loomis Kraal.

Tess took a horse to the range, and for nearly a month they'd rounded up cattle with Alford Cropper and his sons. Ben Finch and Rex Newton had helped, before riding far north to the Yellowstone. From the cattle that Tenbridge's rustlers had missed, there were enough mavericks and yearlings for Lou to build up a small winter herd.

According to county statutes, Lou was still outlawed in Cottonwood County, although a marshal from San Angelo, and a telegram from Barney Ossler in Cuidad

157

Blanco, said there'd likely be no charges brought.

It was on Christmas Eve that Lou and Tess found out that following Clewson's accident, the old man had willed Pasadera to Tess. Later that same night, they sat on the stoop talking it over.

Tess was watching the coyote pups playing along the edge of the gully.

'The ranch is yours by rights, Lou,' she said. 'He didn't even know you were alive when he wrote it.'

'Yeah, I know it, Tess. But this ain't the place for me to settle, not now.'

There was a short silence, then Tess turned and looked closely at Lou.

'You knew about me, didn't you? Before Tenbridge started the talk?' she asked.

Lou nodded and gave a slow, relaxed smile.

'Yeah, I knew. Dad told me. I don't know why he never told you. If he'd known about *me*, that would have been a reason. I mean, who'd want *me* for a half-brother?'

'Why do you say that, Lou?' Tess asked.

Lou thought for a moment. 'You've heard o' the North Reward?'

'Yes, I think so. It was a payment to change sides. Those who took it were sent West, to fight Indians and such, weren't they? To do the government's dirty work?'

'Yeah, that's it, sort of. Well, I was one of those who took that payment.'

Tess looked at Lou with no trace of judgement, and he carried on.

'Texans don't take too kindly to any man who did

that.' Lou clenched his fists, and turned his face to the night sky. 'But they won't be Texans who were forced to waste away in their own filth. It was the likes of Chimm who stole clothes from our backs. We were starved until we fell into our own dirt pits. I had the will to live, Tess.'

Lou stopped talking and Tess thought it was the pain of remembering.

'How long did you do that work for?' she asked.

'A year. I carried mail, raced the telegraph for two years after that. Somethin' to do with runnin' fast an' lonesome, I guess.'

'Well, there's no "sides" any more, Lou. It's all Union administration now. You just started in a bit early. Besides, you've paid for any wrong you *might* have done. It's time to put all that behind us.'

'Hmmm. I'll wager there's few in Cottonwood County who'll see it that way.' Lou bent to scrape up snow from the stoop beside him. 'It'll be a while before this county's right fit to live in, Tess,' he said, looking up at the girl's face. 'All considered, there's not a lot to stay for.'

'Not a lot to leave then,' Tess suggested, quiet and meaningful.

'Wonder how much those few cattle'll bring?' Lou mused. Then he added seriously.

'There's a few thousand dollars in the Cattlemen's Bank. That's enough to start up a business . . . a peace-loving, family business.'

'When he's in the saddle again, Dooley says he'll help, if we want to start over. But where?' Tess asked, interested.

There was silence for a moment, then Lou lobbed a snowball at the pups.

'When I was in Red Bluff, I met a man who called himself Sweet Dog Mitcham. He told me there's fortunes to be made in Australia,' he suggested, and they smiled together.